ÉTIENNE'S ALPHABET

ÉTIENNE'S ALPHABET

a novel by JAMES KING

Cormorant Books

Canada Council **Conseil des Arts**
for the Arts   du Canada
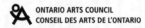 ONTARIO ARTS COUNCIL
CONSEIL DES ARTS DE L'ONTARIO

The publisher gratefully acknowledges the support of the Canada Council for the
Arts and the Ontario Arts Council for its publishing program. We acknowledge
the financial support of the Government of Canada through
the Canada Book Fund for our publishing activities.

LIBRARY AND ARCHIVES CANADA CATALOGUING IN PUBLICATION

King, James, 1942–
Etienne's alphabet / James King.

ISBN 978-1-897151-87-7

I. Title.

PS8571.I52837E85 2010   C813.54   C2010-904411-8

Cover art and design: Angel Guerra/Archetype
Interior text design: Tannice Goddard, Soul Oasis Networking
Printer: Transcontinental

Printed and bound in Canada.

This book is printed on 100% post-consumer waste recycled paper.

CORMORANT BOOKS INC.
215 SPADINA AVENUE, STUDIO 230, TORONTO, ON CANADA M5T 2C7
www.cormorantbooks.com

For Gao Jian
and
Karin Steiner

Autobiography begins with a sense of being alone.
It is an orphan form.

JOHN BERGER

EDITOR'S PREFACE

THE EXISTENCE OF the diary of Étienne Morneau has been known since the day all his remarkable drawings were discovered almost forty years ago. In the past decade, his reputation has soared. In light of this, Madame Beaulieu, the elderly owner of the document, invited me to prepare an edition of it. Reluctantly, I have accepted this assignment. I am a professional art historian and not a literary editor.

Madame Beaulieu and I disagreed on the form in which the autobiography should be presented to the public. She wanted me to place all entries in chronological order and to insert, where necessary, passages linking various parts of the narrative. I refused to do this. Morneau's drawings are always related to the letters of the alphabet. If he decided to write his autobiography as a series of alphabetical entries in the form of a dictionary, that choice must be respected. I also pointed out to her — although she does not really comprehend the matter — that many of Morneau's brightly coloured drawings resemble the collages of Paul Klee. An autobiography that is refractive is perhaps to be expected from this great artist.

She and I almost came to blows on this vexed issue, but we have now resolved our differences. She now agrees that Morneau is best presented in the manner he chose. Besides, the content of this unconventional autobiography — despite its mosaic-like quality — is quite easy to follow. Morneau certainly displayed a slight preference for the order of the alphabet over that of strict chronology, but I find the result, like many aspects of his character, pleasantly teasing. Morneau's transformation from Bank Teller to Artist has so many fascinating twists and turns that the form in which he chose to reveal himself mirrors that curious process.

I had found myself to be more than adequate in preparing the catalogue raisonné published by Princeton University Press four years ago. I have been in a state of constant agitation in preparing this book. Should I annotate some of his references or do all his remarks become meaningful in context? I have simply transcribed the memoir. In academic circles, such an edition is labelled *diplomatic*, the assumption being that it is the kind of approach that is most congenial to the person who wrote it. Even after making this decision, I remain troubled. All of a sudden, Morneau's most intimate thoughts are revealed. He stands naked before the world. Would he have wanted that? Madame Beaulieu says that if he wrote a memoir, he must have intended it to be seen by others. "But," I asked her, "should anyone who wishes be able to see into Étienne's inner being?" She brushed this objection aside: "He had such a beautiful soul — the soul of a child. Readers will be moved and elevated." I am not sure her assumption is correct. We live in a time that cannot abide innocence — so envious are we, in this age of brass, of anyone who passes through life without being corrupted.

Morneau died on 12 October 1967 in his thirty-fifth year. He was a tiny man (very slight — about 5′ 5″ in height, 125 pounds in weight). For nearly seventeen years he worked as a teller at various branches in Toronto of the Royal Bank. Many would consider him an unusual or strange person; most would label him an eccentric.

The facts of his life are easily established. He was found abandoned outside an orphanage in Montreal on December 26 or 27, 1932; his umbilical cord was still attached, and he had obviously been born within a day or two. He remained at the Hôtel Dieu until his seventh year, at which time the Loretto Sisters closed that institution and moved all their charges to St. Bernadette Orphanage in Toronto. Morneau remained there until he was eighteen. His education having been completed, he left the care of the good sisters, obtained a job as a teller at the Royal Bank and took up residence with Madame Beaulieu and her family.

Although he worked at three different branches of the Royal, Morneau resided with the Beaulieus the remainder of his life. He was a solitary man of regular habits. He left for work at seven o'clock each weekday morning, returned home at half past five, took dinner with the Beaulieus, listened to the radio or, later, watched television with them and then went to bed at ten o'clock. On Saturdays he would perform routine errands in the morning, such as having his hair cut; the afternoons were spent at the Toronto Public Library. Sundays he would read, listen to his radio and take long walks. On Saturday evenings he often went to see a film.

Morneau travelled outside Canada only once, when, as he relates in his memoir, he journeyed to Shanghai on behalf of his employer, the Royal Bank. He describes his adventures in this memoir. That trip seems to have been a major catalyst in his decision to commence his now-celebrated drawings. He began them shortly after his return to Canada.

Although Morneau never mentioned his drawings to Madame Beaulieu, she vaguely knew about them because — when cleaning his room on Saturday mornings — she noticed the presence of colour pencils on his desk. Later, the corrugated cardboard boxes slowly began to fill his room. At the end of his life, there were fourteen such boxes numbered in sequence. Each of the boxes contained about one hundred drawings, obviously placed in the order in which they were completed.

Until the day the artist died, Madame Beaulieu knew nothing of the contents of the boxes. She sometimes moved the boxes slightly in order to clean the room; she dusted them, but she never opened them. She was curious, but she respected her tenant's privacy.

On the day after she found Morneau's lifeless body, Madame Beaulieu began to inspect the contents of the mysterious boxes. Although she is the first to admit that she knows little about art, their beauty overwhelmed her. She had been crying over the loss of Morneau, but the discovery of the pictures absolutely overwhelmed her. Having no idea of the hidden treasures in her house, she was filled with a deeper and more poignant sense of bereavement than she had experienced the previous day. She also had to contend with the fact that an autopsy had to be performed. That procedure revealed that Morneau had an undiagnosed heart defect that had caused him to stop breathing.

Morneau's room was stripped bare a few days after he died. There were two reproductions on the walls — Van Gogh's *Starry Night* and a jungle landscape with tiger by Rousseau. There were seven suits in his closet — all purchased from Eaton's — along with a dozen neckties, eight white business shirts, three or four pairs of jeans, and an assortment of coats. The clothes were donated to the Saint Vincent de Paul Society. Next to the typewriter were a dictionary and a thesaurus; there were about five library books. Morneau's bank book showed total savings of $2,113.37.

About a month after Morneau died, Madame Beaulieu wrote to the Art Gallery of Ontario about the drawings. A curator responded by telling her that the "remains" were probably of little or no interest. A resolute woman, Madame Beaulieu insisted the curator meet with her; she took along a sample of fourteen drawings, one from each box. The rest is history. Three weeks later, the curator visited the house, examined the contents of each box, and later informed her superiors that she had discovered the existence of — to use her exact words — "a primitive artist of undoubted genius." Subsequently, the drawings were moved to the AGO and donated to the gallery by the Beaulieu family.

Morneau's memoir can be dated with reasonable precision. In the spring of 1966, he purchased a used Underwood, a monster of a thing, according to Madame Beaulieu. The clicking noise of the machine could be heard by the Beaulieus on Saturday and Sunday afternoons. The surviving manuscript was begun, according to Morneau's preface, on 26 December, 1966 — the day he turned thirty-four — and the last entries were made just before the author's death the following October. Although there are pencilled additions and corrections, it seems certain to me that most of this autobiography was written sequentially. The letters A–C, for example, describe Morneau's childhood and teenage years, and the subsequent entries follow a loose chronology. I am of the opinion that the last entries were written on the day Morneau died. The three letters that Morneau pasted into his memoir are reproduced just as they appear.

I believe Morneau found the ideal form in which to "paint" his self-portrait, but I realize that the readers of his autobiography must be at liberty to reach their own conclusions about this matter.

Stephen Chambers

PREFACE

FOR THE PAST six months I have tried to write an account of my life. This has been a thankless task. I have written five pages, not even a thousand words. There has to be more to me, I tell myself constantly, but I have found nothing to add. In fact, I subtracted almost two hundred words before I tore my miniature autobiography into tiny shreds. Today, on my thirty-fifth birthday, I have decided to make entries in the form of a dictionary in the hopes of capturing reflections of myself. Only in this way will I be able to bring my own life into focus.

A

A. Two converging lines firmly joined by a third. A nice solid beginning. A handsome yet unprepossessing shape. Ornate but subdued.

A knows everything there is about the importance of coming first. In its case, the first shall be first: A-1, A-okay. Despite its marked superiority in any kind of list, A carries its role well — it does not rub its pride of place into the faces of its colleagues. A very considerate citizen to its fellow letters.

AARDVARK: Charming-looking little creatures with built-in suits of armour. In the evolutionary scheme of things, human beings were deprived of this protection, although nothing, I suppose, could shelter us from our real predators — sorrow and misfortune.

ADENOIDS AND TONSILS: Removed when I was six years old. A grainy grey December rain streaked down over the playground from which seven of us were summarily removed by Mother Superior. "You seven, come with me. The doctor is in the infirmary to look at your throats. We've had too many sore throats this winter and so we're going to do something about it. We're going to the expense of having those two troublemakers removed." I was startled. Who was being expelled? When she saw the look of confusion that filled my face, she laughed. "We're having your tonsils and adenoids removed. It will take only a few seconds." I was still perplexed, but I marched along at the front of the group that filed behind her.

Sister Nurse was there to welcome us. She indicated that we should strip to our underwear and then lie down in the six beds lined up in a row. It was only about dinnertime, but the windows in the room were covered to prevent light from entering. I could hardly see the nun and the other five children. "The doctor will visit you in turn. He is a nice man. Afterwards, there'll be a special treat for each of you." We dutifully followed her instructions to be still and awaited the arrival of the doctor. I was patient but anxious. I wondered if I would ever walk out of this shadow-filled room. Even at my tender age, I wondered if I was preparing to meet death.

That day I was especially frightened when I saw the usually genial Doctor Newman. He was dressed in what looked like green pyjamas. That did not bother me. What I did not like was the fact that his head was covered and that a white mask hid his nose and mouth. Sister then placed a white mask over her face.

The room was in darkness. The two shadowy figures walked over to me. I think I screamed, but Sister assured me I had nothing to be fearful of. "This is a humdrum procedure. You will be perfectly all right, Étienne." I remember sucking in my stomach, my body's preparation for uttering some sort of cry for help. While I was doing this, doctor and nurse moved quickly. She placed a cloth over my nose, and I remember a sickly sweet smell. When I looked up at my two tormentors, they seemed twice their usual size. Above their heads, the ceiling was as high and wide as the sky. Then darkness. The next thing I recall was being handed a huge bowl of chocolate ice cream as a reward for being a good boy. I greedily devoured the peace offering at the same time I was aware my throat was very sore. "You and the others will sleep here tonight, dear, and you will be yourselves in the morning." This statement was issued as a command, not a peace offering for the mutilations we had just undergone.

ALCHEMY: Turning brass into gold. Alchemists were consummate tricksters who played upon human greed and credulousness. The oldest scam in the history of the world: something for nothing. An artist or writer can, if he is not cautious, become such a faker as he attempts to extract something precious from his inner chaos.

ALLURE: Well before I learned to read, the letters of the alphabet would appear as free-floating forms before my amazed eyes. For instance, the letter b would begin in lower case and then become a capital B; suddenly it would *b* or **b**. The letter might start as a bright yellow and then turn a deep purple and afterwards a hazy pink. As a child I did not know the names of the various typefaces, but I could see the letter B in what I later knew was sans serif, and then watch it transform itself into Times Roman. My dreams were also filled with the letters forming words in various fonts and colours.

When I was taught to read at the age of five, the black forms on the page would float mysteriously before me and whisper their meanings. The word *chair* would turn itself into the shape of that object and then whisper its meaning and pronunciation to me. "You learn very quickly, Étienne," an astounded Sister Magdalena assured me. When I told her my secret, she did not seem startled: "You obviously have a very active imagination, my boy." I did not divulge any more about my precociousness, nor did I inform her that my *chair* could become an overly stuffed Victorian, then a wooden object of the Bauhaus persuasion and then an elegant mahogany specimen of Chippendale. To my surprise, none of my classmates shared this facility.

ALPHABET: Letters obviously hold the entire world together. Otherwise, there is no order, no language, no significance. When I felt compelled to begin making my strange drawings, I decided to tie each of them to one of the twenty-six letters in the English language. I never gave a title to any of the pictures but all you have to do is look at the letter inscribed on a drawing to make an accurate guess as to its subject matter.

One of my peculiarities is my attachment to all kinds of lists: Lists of Things to Do, Lists of Books to Read, Lists of Appointments. If I did not make such compilations, my life would have no purpose or meaning. I would accomplish nothing. Once, at work, Maria, a fellow teller, advised me to let go. "Steve, be a free spirit. Go with the moment!" The astounded look on my face silenced her. "I didn't mean to hurt your feelings. Sometimes I think you're too attached to unimportant things." I did not bother to point out that she was always asking me to balance her till at the end of the day. In our work, careful attention to detail is the key to success.

Maria, like most of my fellow employees, was insensitive to the fact that my name is Étienne, not Stephen. On my second day on the job, someone remarked, "Étienne is French for Steve, right?" I explained that this was both true and untrue. In French there is also the name Stéphan. That information was ignored. Ever since then I have — despite my requests to the contrary — been Steve at the Bank.

I have a penchant for facts. No doubt about that. Once, during the middle of an examination by a physician, I noticed the acronym "OCD" in large red capital letters next to my name. At first, I thought this was some sort of classification system by which patient records were filed. A few days later I looked up the anagram at the library and discovered that it stood for Obsessive Compulsive Disorder. Sufferers from this ailment, according to the reports I read, often wash their hands twenty times a day, so convinced are they that lurking germs are constantly jumping on them. I resolved to confront this doctor during my next visit, but was too cowardly to do so when the occasion presented itself.

ANIMALS and BIRDS: In my drawings these creatures are exhibitionists. Bears drunk with grapes reeling on the branches of elm trees; caribou bathing in dark, sombre lakes; black, red and grey squirrels frolicking in thick foliage; mockingbirds flying down to feed on strawberry patches; green parrots showing off their yellow heads; crimson-tinged woodpeckers and fire-bright cardinals competing for the tops of cypresses; hummingbirds feasting on blue and purple flowers.

ANGELS: I admire the majestic strength and austere beauty of archangels and seraphim. They are worthy companions of God. However, my heart has always been drawn to the cherubim and, especially, the *putti*, those winged toddler-like beings who hover near and protect the baby Christ.

ANNA: Such a beautiful, simple name, perhaps the perfect name for a *putti*.

APPEARANCES: They are not really deceiving. When I was tiny — six or seven years old — I conceived of every person I encountered as a list. For example,

1. female
2. tall
3. brown eyes
4. no hair visible
5. wimple
6. black skirt
7. black shoes

8. red face
9. no smile

In that way I knew this was Sister Mary Elizabeth, the bad-tempered nun who taught me in Grade Three. Even as a teenager, I thought this way all the time. In recent years I have managed to move away from the construction of these lists. "Étienne, you must avoid thinking this way," I admonish myself.

ASSISI, ST. FRANCIS OF: At the Orphanage, he was not much reckoned in comparison to St. Francis Xavier, one of the seven original Jesuits, who searched for converts in India, Malacca, the Moluccas, Sri Lanka and Japan. The nuns and priests taught us to emulate this man of enormous energy and great courage. They wanted us to be tough in confronting all the vexations with which life would present us.

One day, I confessed to Sister Marguerite that I preferred the animal-loving St. Francis to his namesake, the rugged missionary. I was afraid that this revelation might anger her. Instead, she smiled. "There are two things about you that I shall never forget, Étienne. First: your eyes cannot be described as blue. They are a deep violet. I have never seen such a wonderful colour in anyone's eyes. Second: you are both a gentle and generous creature. Never forget that."

ASYLUM, as in INSANE ASYLUM: My word for the two orphanages in which I was incarcerated. Actually, I am being a bit unfair. The one in Montreal was a large — some would say spacious — Gothic monument. Not an ornate example of that architectural style. The wood around the large portal and the windows was a pale blue, giving the building a slightly friendly look. I think it had four — possibly five — storeys.

In Toronto everything was different. That monstrous structure I remember all too well. St. Bernadette's was newly and badly built in what I would term "Art Deco Institution" style. The dining room, the school, and the nuns' residence comprised the front of the building, whereas there was a wing on each side, one for the boys, the other for the girls. The windows — trimmed in a kind of red plastic — and roof leaked badly for the ten years I lived there. The corridors were filled with noxious fumes — ones I could both see and smell. The rooms were low-ceilinged and vast: twelve children crammed into each dormitory.

I have another memory: the reception room in Montreal was crowded with armoires and other antiques, while the one in Toronto contained black filing cabinets. In Montreal, the two large sofas where visitors could sit were badly frayed, their stuffings tumbling out on to the ground; in Toronto, there was nowhere to sit, a reflection of the fact that few outsiders ever ventured inside the doors.

Hate is a strong adjective to describe one's attitude to a building, but I retain resentful feelings about my first home in Toronto.

ATTENTION: Something I evidently lacked as a teenager. I was an outstanding student in grades One through Eight. For instance, I was a wiz at memorizing the multiplication tables, and I had instant recall of any fact imparted by a teacher. I was the joy of most of my teachers but was considered a "browner" by most of my classmates because my hand was always waving in the air to answer any question posed by a teacher. If a fellow student got something wrong, I did not hesitate to yell out the correct response. One particularly gratifying day, the usually kindly Sister Mary Gregory, with a hint of a macabre smile, attempted to demonstrate to my peers that my talents were finite. "I bet you can't do this one, little smarty pants! Write it down if you need to: one hundred plus one forty-eight, minus one forty-two, plus ten million, minus three, times twenty, times ten." She was not pleased when I calmly and instantly informed her that the answer was 2,000,020,600.

In Grade Nine I fell apart. Algebra and geometry were realms completely closed to me. I somehow managed — despite considerable effort — to get every problem with which I was presented wrong. Latin was another foreign land. I could do simple tasks, like decline agricola — the word for farmer — but the conjugating of verbs, especially the irregular ones, was beyond me. At first, my teachers accused me of sitting on my laurels and not "applying" myself.

This was untrue.

Students whom I had previously surpassed went ahead of me. I heard one teacher say to another: "We don't know anything about the origins of most of those entrusted to us. I fear Étienne's bad seeds have now come to fruition."

I remained a good student of literature and art, but I was a miserable dunce in everything else. At the age of eighteen, the principal — Father Callaghan — informed me that I would be "retired" from further study.

B

B has a slightly pompous air to it. Can be said to look like two large bellies extending themselves from a straight line. Or a straight line with two handsome bulges. My Bs are often a blistering yellow. It is not one of my favourite letters.

B lives in the shadow of A and despises its early bird companion. I can well understand its many problems in self-identity: Plan B.

B-girls are decidedly sordid, but there will be always be a place in my heart for B-movies: they are so determinedly cheap-looking and badly acted that they put real emotions on display.

BANKS: At the age of eighteen, I left the world of orphanages for the confines of banks. I must admit that their regularity — the confined working spaces, the glass tables at which the customers prepare their slips, the marble countertops, and the fact that every bank is basically the same as any other bank — comforts me.

Except for a brief period, I have always been a teller. I am renowned as the employee who has never made a single mistake in his daily tallies — in fact, my fellow tellers always ask me to help them balance their books. Despite my aptitude for my work, I have never been promoted.

"You are not the kind of person who can manage others, old chap," one manager told me. "You have no interpersonal skills," another remarked. "You understand numbers but have not the slightest idea about people," another proclaimed within earshot of everyone else in the Bank. In truth, I like my job. I do it easily and competently. I don't require any more money for my simple needs.

BANK MANAGERS: These people vary enormously in character. Mr. Smiley was choleric. He made it quite clear that if he had had any say in the matter, no "Frog" would be allowed to work for him. A native of Alberta, he wore a Stetson, a huge silver-buckled belt and cowboy boots to the office. A man of medium height and enormous girth, he wore suits intended for tall, slim men. The vast discrepancies between his clothing and his physique made him look grotesque. I think this disjunction caused the blood in his face to swell and give it a purplish tinge. He was rude to everyone he encountered, even clients who had the misfortune to ask to borrow money. He lectured them on the dangers of careless borrowing and refused most loan requests that crossed his desk. He was soon replaced.

Mr. Smith was kindly. He made a point of meeting with every branch member privately once a month. He was a disappointed man. "I should have been a professor. I wanted to go through for English at university, but my widowed mother insisted I enrol in Commerce. What a dull subject that is. And here I am the warden of this bank." Mr. Smith was so tall and willowy that he stooped badly. His face was deeply etched in vertical and horizontal lines competing with each other for supremacy. He was reputedly a soak. "You are a very diligent employee, Stephen. I have never encountered anyone so remarkably dedicated to his job." He then commented on the weather: it was a blustery March morning. "You have little chance of advancement here, my boy. You do your job too well. 'Why quarrel with perfection?' — that's the Bank's attitude. If you manage to get a tally or two wrong in the next month or so, there might be hope for promotion. As you know, the Bank has never looked favourably upon those with your ethnic background. Show them they're wrong."

I think Mr. Smith was telling me to be more carefree, although he and I both knew that was an impossible task. At least Mr. Smith did not bother to mention another well-known truism about French-Canadians: they are so attached to their families that they can never be true to an abstract entity such as a Bank. On the subway I once overheard a snatch of a whispered conversation: "They breed like rabbits. The men are only interested in sex — the women in babies."

BASTARD: The legal word used to describe someone like myself. A child born out of wedlock. In the Orphanage, most of the children were bastards and correctly called each other such. For me, it quickly became a meaningless insult.

Although I was of unknown parentage, Sister Bernadette, the cook, informed me that she was certain she had espied my mother the day she abandoned me. An enormously stout, red-faced and good-natured creature, Sister had returned from the market at about three that afternoon, the day after Boxing Day.

"I must admit that my mind was on the prices of cabbages and broccoli, but I noticed a young wisp of a thing — could not have been more that fifteen — walking ten steps or so behind me.

"She was very pretty in a worldly way. Her light brown hair was fashionably curled, her eyes looked to be a sparkling blue, her nose was a most elegant button, and her lips pale and thin. Her coat was made from expensive wool and it had excellent lines. I would have never remembered her except for the fact that her eyes were filled with tears and that she stumbled along uncertainly, as if on the verge of falling over. In any event, I minded my own business and let myself in the front door of the convent. Your little, squalling self was discovered by Sister Margaret a half hour later. We figured you might have been born on December 26, the feast of St. Étienne, the first Catholic martyr."

BEATLES: Their music is filled with nostalgia. Maybe the young people who run after them want to escape the present? The past is a fertile landscape for John and Paul. The plaintiveness of their lyrics is disarming, urging me to explore the lost language of childhood.

BEATRICE: My favourite of all women's names. I have always been enamoured of its soft, caressing sound, but Dante's devotion to Beatrice Portinari, whom he met in about 1274 when he was nine and she was eight, captivated me when I first read about it. She was dressed in a soft crimson cloth, and the boy instantly fell in love with her, thinking of her as angelic. Since they both lived in Florence, the boy tried to catch an occasional glimpse of the girl. They met again nine years later as she walked along dressed in white, flanked by two older women. She turned and greeted him. Her tender salutation filled him with joy.

And betaking me to the loneliness of mine own room, I fell to thinking of this most courteous lady, thinking of whom I was overtaken by a pleasant slumber, wherein a marvellous vision was presented to me: for there appeared to be in my room a mist of the colour of fire, within the which I discerned the figure of a Lord of terrible aspect to such as should gaze upon him, but who seemed therewithal to rejoice inwardly that it was a marvel to see. Speaking he said many things, among which I could understand but few; and of these, this: "I am thy Lord." In his arms it seemed to me that a person was sleeping, covered only with a crimson cloth; upon whom looking very attentively, I knew that it was the Lady of the Salutation, who had deigned the day before to salute me. And he who held her held also in his hand a thing that was burning in flames, and he said to me "Behold thy heart." But when he had remained with me a little while, I thought that he set himself to awaken her that slept;

after which he made her to eat that thing which flamed in his hand; and she ate as one fearing.

Dante never saw the lady again, but she became the inspiration for his verse. Of course, Dante was very impressionable (as are all great artists) and was able to transmute his obsession into poetry. If she had become his beloved, Dante would probably have remained a literary nobody, an obscure footnote in Italian literary history. He obviously paid a heavy psychic price for his obsession, and there is more than a touch of sado-masochism when his unconscious imagines Beatrice reluctantly consuming his heart. But the metaphor rings true. Art is often the product of loss, a substitute for something missing. Dante was hungry for Beatrice's love, and his desire was never sated.

BEAULIEU, MADAME: When, at the age of eighteen, I was taken into her home, she was a young married woman. The narrow, three-storey house, on a small street off Roncesvalles, was in need of a lot of fixing up: the lawn was a collection of rampantly growing, fierce-looking weeds; the wooden porch was about to fall off; the paint around the windows had vanished.

Deep red lips, a small, well-turned mouth, long eyelashes, dark brown eyes. In those days Madame Beaulieu's frame was slim. Her summer frock was made of a fabric that was a riot of red circles and yellow triangles against black; her turban — a decorative accessory she favoured in those days — was also black. When she answered the door, her face was a bit flush — she had just finished breastfeeding her baby. Before we had exchanged a word of greeting, she told me that she, her husband

and two sons had moved to the house only four months before. "This place is very *dishabillé* — please do not let it bother you. We intend to do a lot of fixing up," she stated, as if voicing a promise. As always, she was true to her word.

Curly haired, black-haired and blue-eyed Luc was three, and Jean-Pierre, only six months old, was almost his opposite: his straight, light-brown hair was accompanied by brown eyes. The little boy was eager to please and relieved when he heard me speaking with his mother in French. The baby looked me in the eye and smiled blissfully.

I had only been in the house for ten minutes when the young matron announced: "My two sons like you *beaucoup*." As always, she inserted French words and expressions when speaking in English; she never used English when speaking in French.

Even then I knew Madame was telling me that she approved of me and would be happy to have me stay. She showed me the first two floors but told me to walk up to the third floor by myself. That was her way of allowing me to gather my thoughts and to decide whether I really wanted to live there.

The room on the third floor — a window at each end — was large and spacious; it even had its own bathroom. I had never seen such a big living space. I could have all of this, I told myself at the same time I congratulated myself on my good fortune. The single bed was a bit small for the enormous room, but I coveted the bureau and desk and armchair that would be only for me.

BEAULIEU, MONSIEUR: His given name is François, but he is always called Frank. A small, muscular man. Perhaps two inches shorter than myself. He hardly ever speaks, but he is not the strong, silent type. He is a brooder: his brow is always tightly knotted.

Frank had been born in Fall River, Massachusetts in a section of that town that was completely French-speaking. His mother and father had been born in Quebec and emigrated to the States in search of factory work when the farm they owned could no longer support them. As a child, Frank longed to return to his parents' native land; in his early manhood, factory after factory in Fall River closed its doors. He took that as a signal to sneak one night across the border into Canada. In Quebec jobs of any kind were difficult to come by in the late 1940s and so he drifted to Toronto, where he finally found work as the janitor at a Catholic grammar school.

Caretaker would be the more appropriate job title. He repairs everything that needs fixing as well as undertaking all kinds of renovations and additions to the school and its grounds. Although his work leaves him exhausted on weekday evenings, he remains gently amiable to his family and me. While we watch television, he smokes his pipe and then dozes off. At about nine o'clock, he gets to his feet, surveys everyone in the living room, nods goodnight and then makes his way to bed.

Madame makes all the decisions — financial and emotional — in her family, Frank happily deferring to her in all things. In more ways than one, I suspect, Frank is handy. He attends the house meticulously; he has handsome children, the faces of each bearing a strong resemblance to his.

BEAULIEU (les fils): Luc was three years old when I met him; Jean-Pierre was a small infant when I moved in with the Beaulieus; Paul came along two years after Jean-Pierre. The colouring of the three children is different: Luc slight and dark; Jean-Pierre pudgy with mouse-brown hair; Paul tall and redheaded. All three are mild-natured, almost as if they had inherited their mother's disposition rather than her looks.

BEAUPRÉ, STE. ANNE DE: I wonder if my visit to that lady's shrine on the St. Lawrence was the beginning of the end of my adherence to Catholicism. At the time, I was five years old. All of us orphans had been guaranteed a special treat. The bus ride would be almost five hours but, at the end, we would see wonders that would make us forevermore "devoted servants" of God.

That promise would, under any conditions, have been a difficult one to keep. The temperature that August day was almost 100, and many of my companions became carsick quite soon after we set off. The stench and the humidity were overpowering, but I tried to put those mundane concerns aside. In my mind's eye I could behold the ancient pilgrimage site — over three hundred years old — built by sailors who often became shipwrecked off Île-aux-Oeufs; I thought of the Virgin Mary's kindly mother, the patron saint of sailors, after whom the Basilica was named; I remembered that I would be able to feast my eyes on the only copy of Michelangelo's *Pietá* outside the Vatican; I knew the place was famous for all the miracles that had been performed there. As soon as we arrived, I comforted myself, my ordeal would be over, and I would be rewarded for my patience.

Before we were permitted to enter the Basilica, we were taken to the small museum that housed a finger bone and wrist bone of the site's patron. Many of my fellow inmates giggled and made rude remarks at these small relics, which were almost impossible to see because each was encased in a huge treasure box and swathed in purple velvet. A bit later, not one of us made a sound, because our breaths were suddenly taken from us as we were ushered into the main door of the Basilica and saw two huge pillars of crutches, walking sticks, canes and braces.

Those remnants were supposed to prove that miracles had taken place, that Jesus's grandmother had interceded on behalf of the sufferers, who gladly left their no longer needed "appliances" (as a nearby sign labelled them) behind. My eyes were drawn to the twenty or so wheelchair-bound persons who had been parked near the pyramids. The face of one young woman was emaciated; she was scarcely more than a skeleton. Several other men and women had facial tics; some screamed in agony — this was obviously the closest they could get to praying.

Finally, my attention was seized by the small boy whose wheelchair was at the outer edge of the periphery. I could only see the back of his head and so I moved closer to take a good look. He must have noticed what I was doing because he turned as if to greet me. His tiny face was wizened; he had a few patches of hair on his head; he was badly dressed; he smelled. He attempted to focus his eyes on me but finally gave up. I could see that, secure in his belief that I was offering to be his friend, I could see that he was trying to smile. I wanted to touch his hand in some gesture of sympathy, but I was quickly shooed away by one of the nuns from our orphanage.

Sister Mary was only doing her job. I had no reason to be angry with her. At the back of my mind that day, it must have dawned on me that a religion that dangles false hopes in front of its believers was beneath my contempt.

BEAUPRÉ, MADAME: The mother of Madame Beaulieu and her younger sister, Isabelle. Big of girth is this woman, but she has an equally large heart. Sometimes she pretends to be harsh, but the warm, bearlike embraces she bestows on her grandsons betrays her. She obviously disapproves of Isabelle, with whom she is forced to live in Montreal. Whenever her youngest child does or says something particularly obnoxious, the mother shrugs her shoulders as if to signify she is not related to this lunatic. At such moments, she winks at me.

BEAUPRÉ, MADEMOISELLE: About twice a year Tante Isabelle, sometimes accompanied by her mother, puts in an appearance, usually for about two weeks. During this time Frank Beaulieu — who is devoted to his mother-in-law — becomes even more uncommunicative than usual and is known to skip meals and frequent public houses. When he returns from those places, he is the gentlest, friendliest soul imaginable. Isabelle summarily informs him that his breath stinks of alcohol.

Tante Isabelle is of the opinion that her sister could have chosen a much better spouse — and she often forces this observation on her sibling. "What about Raymond? Or Lucien? Both better-looking and both successful businessmen." The fact that she had never married is never thrown back in Isabelle's face by her tactful older sister.

Isabelle is taller, more angular than Madame. Her hair is a carefully orchestrated mass of curls. Scarlet lipstick emphasizes the curvaceous shape of her lips. As a result of an illness in childhood, she lost her left eye, which has been replaced by a perfectly fitted glass one. Only with careful observation can the false eye be detected by the casual observer.

Isabelle's athletic figure can be attributed to the fact that she has a factory job that requires her to be on her feet all day. On top of that, she eats, she is always claiming, like a bird. Monsieur Beaulieu once observed that she might not consume much food but that she chops away at what is on her plate like a demented woodpecker.

Tante Isabelle adores her three nephews. She loathes me. To my face she is civil, but I overheard her lambasting her sister for taking me in.

"You must be out of your mind to allow such a strange creature into your home."

"He is a poor orphan."

"You have no idea of who his parents were. His father could have been a criminal, a murderer even. His mother could have been a woman of the streets."

"No matter. He himself is a kind, gentle fellow."

"I do not like the way he speaks. He talks like a robot — like some sort of mechanical man. When I ask him a question, he does not answer me at once. He mulls over what he is going to say."

"He is a sensitive youngster. He is thinking of what you have said and is trying to make the best response. He wishes to please you."

"Nonsense. He is an automaton. What if he becomes deranged? You should not allow such a person near your children." Breaking into English, she warned her sibling: "Your advantage will be taken."

"The boys like him." Madame uttered this statement and then changed the subject. Isabelle then launched into a diatribe against their absent mother, who, she claimed, "was becoming more and more impossible to deal with."

"She contradicts everything I say," Isabelle claimed.

"Maman is a person of firm opinions and so are you," Madame diplomatically assured her. "That is why you fight. She looks after you very well: prepares all your meals, cleans the apartment, and does all the grocery shopping."

Isabelle took no comfort in what her sister told her: "You don't understand. I have never had my own life apart from Maman."

BENOIT: Without doubt, the most mischievous of all my orphan compatriots. After we made our First Communion, the males were all trained to serve as altar boys. We had to set out the priest's vestments, make sure there were enough hosts and wine, and respond in Latin at appropriate moments. Early in the morning, this is a tedious and unrewarding way of spending one's time. Benoit, who was a bit of a glutton, was furious that he had to perform this activity on an empty stomach. To compensate himself for the inconvenience inflicted upon him, he arrived sufficiently early to eat four or five unconsecrated wafers and drink a half glass of wine. His face was so angelic — and he was such a consummate actor — that his thieving went undetected.

BERYL: My most eccentric customer. She would never use any teller but me. "Sonny boy, you're my good luck charm!" Beryl always arrived at our branch ten minutes before the doors were to be closed for the day. "My pal George tells me his jalopy will be roadworthy tonight, and we're off to Woodbine. There are some good little ponies trotting — some old favourites. They've never come in for me before, but these old bones of mine tell me I'm going to hit the jackpot tonight." She would then present me with a withdrawal slip for ten or twenty dollars — a significant portion of what she referred to as her "life savings." Then she would, to use her word, caboodle.

I don't think Beryl ever had a good day at the races. Her savings became more and more depleted. Deposits were a rarity. I knew that Beryl worked as a cleaning lady at one of the men's residences at the University of Toronto, but I had never encountered her on the street. One sunny spring morning, when I had decided to spend my lunch hour exploring the neighbourhood, I espied across the street an excessively old lady walking a West Highland White.

This woman's medium-length hair was completely dishevelled, her face indented with vertical lines, her gait abrupt and unwieldy. Her clothing was a mishmash of purple, yellow and orange threads. Suddenly, this creature began to cross the road in my direction. "Sonny boy, it's you!" I stopped to wait her arrival and noted that the dog — whose name was Eddie — was, unlike his owner, meticulously groomed.

I feebly explained that I was talking a stroll. "You must come over for a visit!" she said. "I insist!" I explained that I did not have much time to spare. "That's no problem! I live right here. Perfect time for a quick cuppa!" The semi-detached building to which she referred was, like its occupant, in a state of advanced decay. No paint remained on its wooden surface, huge chunks of bricks had fallen away, several windows were broken or cracked.

With some misgiving, I agreed to cross her threshold, but I must admit to having felt a bit like Hansel entering the witch's cottage. The small hallway was filled with piles of the *Telegraph* and *The Racing Times*. I followed my hostess towards the kitchen, which was filled with piles of dirty dishes and the smell of rotting food. She quickly filled a kettle, brought the water to a boil, opened the fridge door and managed, with considerable difficulty, to find an almost empty bottle of milk. She then grabbed a small tray on which she placed the now tea-filled cups and saucers, two spoons, and a milk jar. "We'll wait in my room for the tea to steep." She then handed me the tray and told me to follow her. With some difficulty, she fidgeted with the key to the padlock, which guarded against unauthorized intruders. "I have to do this because otherwise they would steal all my earthly possessions." The "they" were her boarders, most of whom failed to pay their rent in a timely manner, thus causing the owner of the house to seek redress from his resident-manager.

Beryl's room had a messy simplicity. Every possible surface was covered with white sheets and pieces of white cloth. Since the window shade was drawn against the sunlight, the long strip of florescent lighting over the bed made the room resemble a stage set appropriate for a play by Beckett.

"Do you take sugar with your tea?" Beryl asked. I confessed I did. "Wait a sec, then." Then she threw herself to the floor and proceeded to dive under the bed. A few moments later, she emerged with a tattered Dominion Sugar bag, which she handed to me. "Help yourself." After I did that, she told me that her back was torturing her. Could I return the bag to where it lived? "Otherwise one of them will break in here and steal it." I agreed and made my way into that subterranean region, which was filled with boxes of macaroni and crackers and jars of jam and jelly.

Once I was standing upright again, Beryl informed me that she would return to the Bank with me. "I can feel it in my bones. Tonight I'll have ol' George drive us to see the steeds run. I'm going to be very lucky. Meeting you on the street has made my day. I'm always looking for good omens."

BIBLE: The Old Testament is the greatest repository of tales known to man; even the Greek and Roman myths take second place to its stories of creation, destruction, abandonment and cruelty. I admire the angry, headstrong Christ who lashes out at the moneylenders in the New Testament, although I now have doubts about his divinity.

BIRTH: The act of coming into the world. Something we never remember. Perhaps a little bit like death?

Most children are told by their parents about the circumstances of their entry: for instance, their weights and lengths. Boys and girls routinely know if their arrival was difficult or routine. They are sometimes informed if their mothers had a difficult pregnancy, or, for instance, if they had suffered from high blood pressure. Some children even learn if their births were eagerly awaited or direly anticipated.

Many orphans have some idea of the situations that greeted them. I have not been privy to any such details about myself. I know that I was born and almost immediately placed on the doorway of the Orphanage in Montreal. The blanket in which I was wrapped was covered in blood, presumably my mother's mixed with mine. I screamed more loudly than most newborns because — it was judged — I was so cold. "You had a good set of lungs," the Mother Superior informed me years later. "You wanted us to hear you. What a greedy little thing you were! Having gone through all the tedious formalities of arrival, you did not wish to be deprived of life." Of course, she had a broad grin on her face when she uttered these words. Mother Clothilde was a person with a sense of humour.

Obviously I do not remember that infant. These days I sometimes capture in my mind's eye snapshots of the five-year-old Étienne: very small for his age; unfailingly polite; energetic; a day-dreamer. He could never quite fit in with his confreres; he willingly helped the nuns in attending to the babies and toddlers; he looked intently at things, as if possessed of a philosophical turn of mind. This tiny boy never cried, although he was melancholic. I am certain he felt crushed by life but refused to indulge such fantasies.

BLUNDERBUSS: This word for someone who manages to do everything wrong in an almost frenetic way has a comic edge to it. Fiercely red-haired Lucille Ball is my idea of such a person. In her truly loveable but self-centred way, her character Lucy misunderstands or misinterprets what she is told or what she thinks she has seen. As a result of this gross incompetence, she creates mayhem out of a very ordinary domestic existence and, in so doing, reinvents the world around her.

I may love Lucy, but my experience with blunderbusses has not been comic. Sister Patricia Francis — my fifth-grade teacher — was small, squat and bulldog-faced; she had what is often called a choleric temperament. She was a great believer in "womanliness" but, especially, "manliness." The former term was used by her intermittently, the latter all the time. Manly boys were good athletes; their high spirits sometimes led to disobedience but when confronted by authority, they candidly admitted that they had done wrong.

I was obviously not one of the manly boys. One day I went to the local public library and borrowed a copy of a book on Greek gods and goddesses. That evening I was absorbed by the book when Sister pounced upon me.

"What exactly are you reading?"

"A book on the Greek divinities, Sister."

"A book about heathen gods?"

"Yes. Many of the poems we have been reading refer to those myths." I hoped that my use of the word *myths* would show that I didn't believe in the existence of such individuals and therefore disdained their status as gods.

"Let me look at that book!"

I handed her the text and she went through it page by page. Her face blushed, a sure sign that her anger would soon be out of control. "This book is disgusting and should not be in the hands of a young boy. Those men and women are stark naked. Their private parts are shamelessly on display!" (The book was illustrated with photographs of the well-known sculptures.)

"I am removing this book from you and will see that it makes its way out of this institution!"

I realized that no protest would be heard and did not bother to utter one. I sucked my breath in because I knew the accusation that would now be hurled at me. In Sister's world view, the opposite of manliness in a boy was deceitfulness. "You are a very sneaky, underhanded person, Étienne. You have smuggled filth in here and thought that your errant ways would not be detected." I was ordered to bed at once. Sneaks did not require supper.

BOOKS: As a teenager, I was an avid consumer.

The truth is that I am now addicted to picture books and have become less interested in the text-only fiction and non-fiction that grown-ups are supposed to like. Maybe I never quite made the transition from childhood to adulthood — I have never put away my fascination with seeing how an artist translates words into pictures.

As a four-year-old, I would spend hours gazing at picture books and, in a reverie-induced state, would eventually enter their domains, where I spent many happy hours. One afternoon, I gazed for what seemed like hours at a brightly coloured pop-up book, which showed in meticulous detail the inside of a house — basement, ground floor, second floor and attic. A woman was baking in the kitchen while below her a man was making a piece of furniture in his workshop. In my mind's eye, I wandered into that place, inspected all the rooms and wanted to remain behind with those two people, who could, I imagined, look after me. Someone called my name, and I was abruptly brought back to reality. I was profoundly sad the remainder of that day.

For better or worse, pictures — not words — allow me to wander freely in the enchanted world of possibilities.

BOREDOM: The supreme emotional state of orphanhood. Lonely evenings spent reading by oneself. Long, long weekends with nothing to do on Saturday and Sunday afternoons. Sometimes there would be a bus trip on a weekend to a place like the Royal Ontario Museum, but mostly I recall vast stretches of emptiness. Lengthy stints of time in which to think — and become excessively sad.

BROTHER ANDRÉ [1]: The famous one was born in Saint-Grégoire d'Iberville, a town forty kilometres east of Montreal. Orphaned at the age of twelve, he emigrated to New England to work in the mills. In 1867, the year of Confederation, he returned to Quebec, where he became a member of the Congregation of the Holy Cross. He was employed for forty years as the doorkeeper at Notre Dame College in Côte-des-Neiges.

Although Frère André was a languid, sickly looking person and a daydreamer, he began in 1904 the construction of a small chapel on the side of Mont Royal facing the college. He was able to do this because he had acquired the reputation of being a miracle worker. Money poured in to construct the oratory, which was dedicated to St. Joseph, the devout brother's great patron. It was destined to become the largest Catholic church outside Rome.

We were taken to see the oratory in 1938, the year after Brother died. The huge church was still in the process of construction, but we visited the purple and black-silk-lined room where Frère André's heart was preserved in formaldehyde. Then we were escorted to the small cabin where the Brother had lived. Many nights, we were told, he had wrestled with the devil until dawn. His sleepless nights contributed to his always frail health — although he did live until his eighty-first year.

I wish I had never been taken to that grim room — a simple cot, a washstand, a small rag rug by the bed — where the poor man confronted the forces of evil. I was scared that such a sinister force could be let loose on any human being. I resolved to be the best boy possible so that I was not subjected to such an encounter, one I was convinced I would lose.

BROTHER ANDRÉ [2]: Nothing like number 1. He was evidently a reformed alcoholic who, at the age of fifty, embraced the religious life. Although he did not drink spirits any longer, the nuns talked of him with considerable distaste. "It's not that he smokes so much. That I can tolerate. But does he have to spit everywhere?" Our André must have been close to eighty when I knew him. He would grunt perfunctory hellos in the direction of anyone who addressed him, but he pretty much kept to himself.

One day Sister Bernadette informed us that she had received two complimentary tickets in the mail to see Mr. Blackstone, the world-famous magician, that evening. The problem was that not one of the nuns was available to accompany one lucky child to that event. Having made that announcement, she scuttled away.

Being somewhat of a resourceful frame of mind, I asked André if he would accompany me. "I'm sure the Sisters would let me go if you took me." There was no reply. I pleaded with him, but to no avail. That afternoon and evening I imagined how wonderful the magic show would be and lamented my inability to get there. At six-thirty, I was in study hall when a strange man approached me. As he got closer, I realized that André had shaved himself, obviously bathed and was clad in a smart black overcoat. "Well, what are you waiting for? We have to hurry to be there on time!"

André maintained his habitual silence during our tram ride to the city. I could hardly contain myself at the spectacle that was about to enfold before my eager eyes. My overseer did not reply to my chit-chat, but I could see a glint of amusement in his usually unemotional countenance.

As it turned out, we had just about the best seats in the house, only about four rows from the stage. Hardly ever in my life has an event exceeded high expectations. With great charm and considerable boastfulness, tall, angular, moustachioed Mr. Blackstone pulled rabbits out of hats and sawed women in half. The time passed by quickly and rapturously. Towards the end of the second act, Mr. Blackstone pointed at me. "I should like that young man to join me on stage."

André, his face having broke out into a wry smile, urged me forward: "No need to be shy, my boy."

I rose from my seat and headed in the direction of Mr. Blackstone, who merely asked my name and age.

Looking down at me, the magician announced: "This young man is going to assist me this evening in the most difficult trick in my entire repertoire." Pausing for effect, he continued: "Sabrina, bring me the cage." Nodding in her employer's direction, the scantily clad assistant walked off stage and then returned with an enormous bamboo bird cage. She placed it on a table half-way between me and the magician. Inside the cage were five canaries. "Perhaps the young man will be kind enough to put his hand in the cage and attest to the fact that these creatures are alive and well?" He then advanced towards me, pointed me in the direction of the cage and opened its door. Following his instructions, I placed my hand in the cage whereupon one of the tiny birds landed on my hand, looked at me quizzically and then darted off. There they were: splendid specimens of the canary race. Two were a pale yellow, one an orange yellow, and the others red yellow. My inspection over, the Maestro asked me to step back. "Étienne, you attest to the fact that these are five living avian creatures before you?" I nodded in assent.

Blackstone then stood on a chair, asked Sabrina to hand the cage to him, and asked her to drape the cage with a purple silk covering. At that point, the magician asked me to walk around him. Then he asked me take a second circuit with a pole in my hand to determine if any wires were present above or on the sides of him or the cage. I did this. "You are the best assistant ever, my boy. Step back a bit and take your place next to Sabrina."

The magician looked at the audience directly, shook his outstretched hands, and the silk covering fell to the floor. There was no cage; there were no birds.

On the way back to the Orphanage, I confessed to André that I was filled with trepidation about the fate of the birds. I had no idea whether there were alive or dead. I had absolutely no understanding of how Blackstone could achieve this piece of magic. We had seen a miracle.

The elderly man shook his head. "I have no idea of how he accomplished what he did. It looked like a miracle but it was only an illusion. Those birds and their cage are completely safe somewhere." I accepted this assurance, but that night I was deeply frightened. If the Devil could wrestle with Brother André I, how could I be sure that Mr. Blackstone had not signed a compact with Satan that allowed him to perform such feats?

On the following morning, André II gave me his usual gruff greeting. Things had returned to normal.

BULLIES: This is a subject about which I have too much first-hand knowledge. One of my first recollections is of being beaten up by a six-year-old who demanded possession of the building blocks I was playing with. Fred, outraged that I did not wish to surrender the four or five pieces in my possession, gouged the side of my head with one of them. I remember the thick red blood that soon covered every one of the blocks, and being swooped up by one of the nuns and spending the rest of the day in the infirmary.

From that day forward I was teased mercilessly by Fred and his band of thugs, who made sure that their crimes went undetected. Surreptitiously they would remove food from my tray or drink my glass of milk before I could touch it. When the nuns were absent from the playroom, they would swarm around me, threatening dire bodily consequences.

$\mathcal{C}$

C — together with S — is a difficult letter to love. Both of them are arrogant. The C has a simple curve by which it announces its place whereas the sinuosity of the S is like that of the serpent that tempted Eve in Eden. In addition, C seems deliberate in its studied nonchalance. To my eyes, it has a brutal edge, as when it is written as a slash to indicate a mediocre mark on an academic assignment. Like most human beings, I have my measure of pride, but I despise exhibitionists and, in the final analysis, C luxuriates in displaying its vainglory.

The powers of C have been brilliantly exploited by Coca-Cola. The two Cs, in an elegant signature style, seem to open their arms in a warm embrace and even a smile. Seldom has seduction been so perfectly enacted by the letters of the alphabet.

CABBAGES: Detestable. Objects of scorn. At both orphanages, we consumed cabbage at least once a day: cabbage soup, cabbage and potato soup, cabbage salad, coleslaw. The taste is despicable but what is worse is that the odour invades the walls, floors and ceilings of every room, impregnating every object in its wake. That sickly sweet, dank, rotten smell followed me everywhere. As a child, I could not rid myself of it. I bathed frequently — sometimes twice a day — but could not escape. The water smelled of it; my clothes reeked of it. Years later, I encountered a fellow inmate who told me that he shared the same aversion. "It must be part of the condition of orphanhood," he assured me.

Madame Beaulieu was a great admirer of this vegetable. On the day I moved in, she served a cream soup made from it. I ate my portion and told her it was delicious. She smiled in appreciation of my compliment. A day later, she called me aside. In the most polite manner possible, she told me that she had seen me wince when I had downed my first spoonful. She then smiled, indicating that she was waiting for my response. Throwing caution to the winds I confessed everything to her. "*Mon Cher*, I am so happy that you have told me. Never more will a cabbage enter this house!" As always, she held to her word.

CALLAGHAN, FATHER: The head of the Orphanage in Toronto. Although memory is treacherous, I am sure I have an accurate recollection of this Godzilla-like creature. He stood six feet, eight inches tall, was of a firm, slim build and had fingers the size of bananas. His thinning hair stood up uneasily, was constantly filled with bubbles of sweat, and he spent much of his time slicking it back during conversation. His deep-set, hooded eyes always demanded the unswerving attention of whomever he was speaking to.

The move of the Montreal inmates to Toronto distressed him greatly. "You children are intrinsically different from your English-speaking counterparts. Not as intelligent, much more shifty, far less trustworthy," he informed us at our first assembly.

My own particular crime was lack of modesty of the eyes. "I notice, Étienne, that your eyes wander everywhere indiscriminately. The idea never seems to enter your head that you might simply gaze inwardly. Curiosity is both an idle pursuit and a vice."

As I got older and did not do well in school, he accused me of laziness. "This is a characteristic of the French-Canadian male, of which you are an obvious example. You never attain anything in life, Étienne, without hard work. You have always been a daydreamer. Sooner or later you must rid yourself of this form of self-abuse."

CALLIGRAPHY: I have always been able to tell anyone — who would be foolish enough to be interested in such a fact — that, say, 489 multiplied by 1012 equals 494,868. As I have already pointed out, plane geometry remained baroque to me, and I never understood why someone would wish to have an x equal the number 9. My ability to add, subtract, multiply and divide numbers instantly has been useful on occasion at the Bank, but I have always been careful to conceal it lest it provide further evidence that I am some sort of sideshow freak.

With letters and the words they form I have always found a measure of redemption. Sister Magdalena, spurred on by my precociousness, lent me books on calligraphy and provided me with nibs, pen holders and ink.

Within a short period of time, I learned about their various shapes (round, rectangular, extra wide, narrow). I delighted in constructing the serifs, the tiny ticks made as the pen is lifted off the paper. I loved the capital and minuscule letters. Sister was amazed that I soon knew a wide variety of alphabets: Roman, Ornate Gothic, Uncials, Carolingian, Humanist, Italic. On the day I penned a note in Swash capitals (with their dashing extra strokes) tears filled her eyes.

CAMELOT: Not quite as good a musical as Lerner and Lowe's earlier *My Fair Lady*. I hardly ever go to live theatre, but I made an exception to see Robert Goulet, Julie Andrews and Richard Burton at the O'Keefe Centre. I was especially proud of Goulet — one year younger than me, Franco-Canadian in ancestry and raised in Canada — when he sang the boast-filled "C'est Moi" and the haunting "If Ever I Would Leave You" in his manly tenor voice. I heard several of my co-workers speaking rapturously of what they called his "golden" voice.

CANADA: Next year we will celebrate one hundred years of Confederation. I don't think I have any real idea what Canada is — I don't think many of my fellow citizens know how to define the word with any precision. A loose assemblage of provinces? A nation with little sense of shared purpose? A large land mass north of the United States that is not the United States?

I was born in Montreal and my first language was French. As a young child, I learned English as a classroom subject and spoke it with a decidedly French accent. When I arrived in Toronto, I — like the other children who accompanied me — was instructed to speak only in English so that any trace of a French accent would eventually disappear.

The other overwhelming concern was the use of hands when speaking. The French often wave their hands when talking — it's a way of getting the right words to come out and to give emotional accompaniment to them. Now, we were instructed never to employ our hands when speaking. In fact, we were punished if we did so. "Boys who use their hands when speaking are sissies," we were further told. If we did not erase our French ancestry from our behaviour, we were warned, we would be ostracized. "You will be seen as 'funny' and not fit in." The last thing any of us wanted was to appear odd and so we — most more easily than me — followed the injunction.

I live in a household in Ontario where French is spoken by my landlords, although their three sons prefer English. Quebecers are often referred to as "frogs," and whenever Quebec makes any sort of demand of the rest of Canada, people in Toronto shake their heads and mutter, "I thought we won the war, but those sons-of-bitches refuse to admit it. It's time we showed them who is boss."

At work, I am expected to deal with all customers who speak French — or refuse to speak in English. My co-workers utter this refrain: "They should damn well learn to talk in English. Most of them can speak English but refuse to do so."

What is so special about being an English-speaking Canadian as opposed to a French-speaking one? It seems to come down to a matter of power and who possesses it. If this country is so divided between those who speak two languages, what hope does it have to survive? I shall not be among those celebrating Confederation.

CHARACTER and CHARACTER TRAITS: My personality seems to be a composite of some undesirable traits such as brashness, gangliness, reticence and detachment. If you have such failings, can you be said to have any real character? Do I have enough positive qualities to offset the bad ones?

CHARLES VAN DOREN: Ten years ago we would eagerly watch the young, awkward English professor on the game show *Twenty One*. He quickly became the hero of everyone in the Beaulieu household. Before him, we had to put up with the reigning champion, the unappealing Herb Stempel, who, Madame Beaulieu observed, was an insufferable "know-it-all." He looked like an angry owl, and we prayed for his defeat. Then, a knight in shining armour appeared and bested him.

Madame Beaulieu once remarked that the blond, angular, stoop-shouldered Van Doren reminded her of me. "He is a tall man, which you are not. But, like you, he is someone filled with knowledge, and he is modest, almost to a fault." Our household went into mourning when Van Doren, after two wonderful months, lost to Vivienne Nearing on March 11, 1957.

We forgot about Van Doren in the next two years, until he was accused of having participated in a deception: he had been given, the allegations stated, the answers to all the questions in advance. We believed him when he said, "It's silly and distressing to think that people don't have more faith in quiz shows."

Our faith was crushed when he finally admitted to Congress, "I was involved, deeply involved, in a deception. I have a long way to go. I have deceived my friends, and I had millions of them. Whatever their feeling for me now, my affection for them is stronger today than ever before. I am making this statement because of them. I hope my being here will serve them well and lastingly."

Madame Beaulieu was emphatic: "He is a young man and succumbed to temptation. We must pray for him." I nodded my assent, but even a decade later I still feel stung by his deceit. I was one of his friends; I trusted him. I wonder how many of us have the strength to resist, when offered, the gaudy lures of the world?

CHINA and JAPAN: As a child, I was aware of the geographical location of each country. However, members of both nations were objects of scorn. After the Pacific War, Japan's revitalized manufacturing capacity — especially in cheaply manufactured goods — led to sayings such as: "Easy, easy, Japan-easy."

Vituperation was also poured aplenty on the "slitty-eyed" Chinese. Even as a small boy, I knew it was incorrect to refer to a "Chinaman"; such an epithet was the equivalent of calling someone a bogeyman. Only as a teenager did I realize the full extent to which racism visited upon Orientals was also applied in English Canada to people, such as myself, from Quebec.

Until I was actually forced to visit Shanghai, all that I really knew about that fabled city came from *Le Lotus bleu*, the story of Tintin's adventures there. I did not wish to go to a place filled with rickshaws, opium dens and unsavoury characters. On an almost daily basis, the *Telegraph* was filled with stories about the evil empire Mao and his minions had constructed. I did not wish to be kidnapped and disappear off the surface of the earth.

CHOICES: I was not often hot-tempered as a child, but I did become irate at Mother Clothilde one day over some insignificant matter. Unusual for me, I refused to do what she ordered. "Étienne, you have two choices. Either you do this or you do that!" Was I being precociously philosophical when I bellowed at her, "CHANGE THE CHOICES"?

CHURCH: When I first arrived in Toronto, I explored the city on weekends. I obviously wanted to make myself comfortable in my new environment. I never knew Montreal well, but for me it was a magical assortment of lights, heavy snow in winter, and old, elegant buildings. At first, Toronto seemed a cold and distant place. When I took the streetcar to work, I was surrounded by excessively white-skinned automatons. There was no animation in the faces of my fellow inhabitants; their clothing was in shades of black and white; there were no polite exchanges between customers and clerks at the convenience stores; "thank you" was an uncommon expression.

One Saturday evening when walking along Front Street, I came upon the fish market at Colborne Street. In the dusk my nose was assaulted by the stink remaining from the day's transactions. Then I looked down the lane and was startled by the illuminated clock that bestows its warm glow on the tower and spire of St. James's Church. In a flash, I felt more at home, although I have retained a guarded view of Toronto. For me, it remains a place of possibilities.

CLEANLINESS: Next best thing to godliness. I like ordered environments, although I have had to sacrifice that wonderful state of being in the past ten years. I used to make rigorous efforts in that direction: I made my bed as soon as I arose in the morning; the top of my desk was always precisely arranged: pens, pencils, paper in the correct places. Some people like a neat appearance — an appearance of order — but heap their clothes haphazardly about in closets or chest drawers. I used to be meticulous about such matters before the "great change" began five years ago — as Madame Beaulieu sarcastically, but jokingly, refers to it. "Once upon a time, Étienne, your room was a model I used to show my sons in the hopes they would copy you. Now, I sometimes find a sock under the bed; some Saturday mornings I have to return your shoes to their proper place; the other day there was a necktie on top of your bed."

CLIPPED: This word has been applied to describe me more than once. One manager informed me, "You are always friendly and pleasant to customers, but you give them the impression everything is all business with you. You sometimes work too rapidly, too mechanically. Your *thank yous* and *good mornings* may be accompanied by a smile, but the greetings and the smiles seem forced, as if you are doing everything by rote. In our racket you have to train yourself to act more enthusiastically than you really feel. Otherwise, you're not doing your job properly."

I remain a dismal failure. I like my customers and wish to do the best for them, but I have to practise smiling. In essence, I'm not a good teller because I am not a good actor. Madame Beaulieu has told me several times, "You are a friendly sort, Étienne, but people sometimes think you are too stiff."

CLOCKS: Hold the world together. Time, of course, does not exist as such — it is a figment of our imaginations, a way of applying order where there is none. Yet the division of time into seconds, minutes, hours, days, weeks and years is a comforting illusion. I have drawn so many clocks because they are reminders of the illusory strands that keep us going.

THE COLISEUM: My favourite Toronto landmark. When it opened in 1921 in the west end of the city near the lake, it was the largest building under one roof in the world. It is supremely ornate — a structure that is proud of its elaborate facade and its turrets. Although it looks like a structure built to rule the world, its main purpose is for the exhibiting and judging of livestock at the Canadian National Exhibition at the end of summer and the Royal Agricultural Winter Fair. I like the CNE and have visited it at least a dozen times. The exhibits seem inordinately proud — self-satisfied bulls, cows, horses and pigs — but they probably feel an obligation to live up to the nobility of the building constructed for them.

THE COLOSSEUM: The only school project I ever did really well on. Sister Immaculata told me that she thought I would do an excellent job studying the unbelievable cruelties inflicted upon the Christians in that vile den of torture of ancient Rome. Eagerly I looked up all the many books in our school library dedicated to the injustices inflicted upon Catholics (other denominations of Christianity were considered pagan and so there were no books on them). I learned about all the kinds of fierce combats between various kinds of men called gladiators at the Colosseum; my eyes opened wide and my heart was torn asunder by the pictures of the poor followers of Christ being fed to lions.

I never had the courage to tell Sister that I had been most astounded and moved by an event that had nothing to do with the followers of our religion. Huge beasts were imported to Rome for special events. Once they arrived, those creatures were kept in underground cages. When their turn came, the animals were lifted up to the main floor of the Colosseum by giant elevators. On one occasion, a giant male hippopotamus found himself at one end of the huge stage. He looked around, belched and defecated. Then, about ten minutes later, three lionesses appeared at the other end of the huge stage. They had not been fed for three days and began to stroll back and forth as if in heated conversation. Suddenly, one of them ran at the hippo while the other two followed on her right and left flanks. The hippo killed the animal directly assaulting him by pushing her with his mouth and then stomping on her. He did the same to the one on his left, but his remaining opponent tore the skin off his back in one mighty swoop. His blood flew into the auditorium, liberally sprinkling itself on many spectators. He turned around to kill his remaining enemy, but she was too fast for him. With a mighty leap, she tore at his chest, exposing his heart. There was another huge cascade of blood. The hippo should have been dead, but he used all his considerable bulk to crush his last opponent. Finally, the two beasts lay there, their bodies shuddering. As death overtook them, the audience had the grace to applaud.

Sister told me that I had put tremendous feeling into my composition, but all the emotions I had conjured up were really to do with those poor mammals. She would have labelled me a pagan if I owned up to the real source for my inspired words.

COMIC BOOKS: Strictly forbidden at the Orphanage. Visitors were told not to give them as presents, and we were inspected for contraband at the end of visiting hours. Some of the nuns rebelled against this regulation, but they faced retribution from Mother Superior or Father Master if caught. Copies of *Superman* and *Batman* were highly prized by the boys, but I must admit that I was most attracted to the *Classics Illustrated*, issues of which were only valued by girls with glasses. I did not mind being teased for liking these "sissy" books.

I first read classics like *Ivanhoe* and *A Tale of Two Cities* in these highly abridged, picture-filled versions, and I know my early love of fiction was ignited by them.

COMMUNION: Even as a seven-year-old preparing for his First Communion, I had trouble with the Real Presence. How could I be expected to receive and consume (but never bite into) the Body of Our Lord? I spent many sleepless hours in the middle of the night worrying about that upcoming event. I vowed that I would — as advised — allow the host to melt on my tongue. Of course, in my usual clumsy and forgetful manner, I chomped into the host as soon as it was placed in my mouth. What should have been a day of great happiness was quickly transformed into one of intense sorrow. I found it difficult to conceal my tears.

As a young child I loved Jesus. I was especially taken with the Infant Jesus of Prague. At the Orphanage in Toronto, the statue of the baby had a wide array of costumes — red, yellow, white, purple, black — made of the finest silk. He was easy to adore.

Later, as a teenager, I identified with Christ the revolutionary, the man who ridiculed the Pharisees. I loved memorizing the questions and answers in the Catechism in preparation for Confirmation. I was proud that I knew the whole document by heart. Nowadays, I still attend church every Sunday morning, but I do this out of respect for Madame Beaulieu, a devout believer.

How did I lose my faith? Most of the nuns and priests I knew as a child had my best interests at heart. I never consciously abandoned my religious beliefs but over time my feelings about God the Father, his Son and the Holy Spirit vanished, leaving an empty space. Perhaps I feel that God never gave me anything for which I should be thankful. I am a bit of an ingrate, I suppose, but I cannot, in the final analysis, summon up any enthusiasm for being his child, especially when he is divided into three equal parts like an isosceles triangle.

COMPLIMENTS: This is the nicest I ever received: "You are a man of many hidden talents. The twists and turns in your existence have yet to surface. You combine the child and the adult within yourself — when lightning strikes and sets free your sleeping paper flesh, something glorious will explode, like a stick of dynamite."

CONNECTIONS: "Only connect," E.M. Forster advised. Easier said than done. Isn't life really a series of disconnects?

CONSTANCE: At the age of about forty, she is remarkably pretty. Her cheeks shine deep red, her lips form the most perfect bow I have ever seen, and her head is adorned with a mass of dark brown curls. The redness of her countenance probably owes a great deal to the several glasses of sherry she washes down at lunch. She is a bit stocky in girth, but she is resolutely girlish. Charm is another attribute she possesses in abundance. She listens attentively to what everyone says and asks intelligent questions. She is the epitome of empathy. Yet I am her only friend at the Bank. It took me a while to figure out that any confidences bestowed upon her are soon known to all and sundry. Since I have no confessions to reveal or would be willing to reveal, she and I remained on the best of terms until the day I snapped at her.

CRIB: Strange as it may seem, I slept in one until my sixth birthday. The Orphanage simply did not have enough cots and so one graduated to a bed at a comparatively late stage in childhood. My first memory — I must have been about three years old — is of staring out of the slats one night at dusk; the remaining sunlight created large shadows on the wall. I became so frightened that I wailed uncontrollably. The sister on duty rushed over. Why was I screaming? I couldn't tell her a sensible answer: I'm not sure I knew myself. She shook her hand at me and ordered me to be quiet.

Of course, no toddler with any self-respect will remain in a crib, especially in the morning. My second memory is of a bright Sunday morning in spring. There must have been twenty children in that dormitory, and I remember at least fifteen of us in various stages of climbing out of our individual little prisons. Some were rattling the bars; some were scaling the bars; others landed noisily on the floor. The din was so great that three nuns rushed into the room to discover what was happening. When they discovered what we were doing, they shrugged their shoulders: "The little monkeys have contracted spring fever!"

CUTE: In my first five years, a crucial concept. If a two- or three-year-old orphan smiles or makes cute with a childless couple interested in adopting him, he has a much improved rate of success than a child who is, say, withdrawn, taciturn or merely quiet. I could never make what the nuns called a "happy face" when a husband and wife came to see me. These visitors seemed dissatisfied with life. They wanted to have children of their own, couldn't, and were reduced to settling for someone else's discards or left-behinds. Perhaps they bore an unconscious grudge against the children they sought to take into their homes.

After four unsuccessful visits from prospective parents, the nuns informed me I must improve my manners or be left behind. "You are a very handsome little boy, Étienne. Many childless couples are looking for good sons." I always said "thank you" for their advice but secretly shrugged my shoulders. I did not wish

to take up residence with any of these people. Aware, even at a
tender age, of the many obstacles that would block my path, I
resolved to confront them on my own.

D

With **D** you know exactly where you stand. Its character is stolid. Its central long line is definite, establishing its place near the beginning of the alphabet. From that central line it reaches out with one long curved line to the curved space that completes it with the hint of a flourish. The straight and the not-so-straight conjoined. There is humility to a **D**: it knows it needs a curve to complete itself.

DEATH: Although I would never describe Madame Beaulieu as a carefree person, she greets every day as a welcome friend. She is occasionally a bit grumpy with her spouse, but she always bestows smiles on her sons and me as if it were impossible we could do anything wrong. I think that psychologists call this "unconditional love."

One afternoon when I arrived home from work, she was sitting by herself in the living room, her cup of tea at her side. When I sat down to chat with her, I noticed that the edges of her eyes were swollen. She had been crying. I asked her what was wrong.

"Nothing. *Mon cher*. I have been thinking of my old life."

She then told me that her own childhood had been a very happy one, although she had had to leave school at the age of fourteen to help her parents make ends meet; she had worked long six-day weeks at a mill, something she did for ten years before she met Frank and married him. All those years had passed by in a whirl because she had been happily attached to her parents. "My parents thought I was something of a wild girl because I liked to go dancing on Saturday nights, but they knew they could always count on me to be virtuous."

The great sorrow of her early life had been the death of her brother, Jean-Baptiste, three years older than Madame. The two had been inseparable as young children, and she had been distraught when he joined the American Navy at the age of seventeen. She remembered the postcards he had sent from various foreign locales; she still had a photograph of him taken in a large square in Havana, giant palm trees in the background. When he was home on leave, they spent as much time as possible together.

Then came 1942. When he left home that spring, he hinted that his ship might be heading for the Pacific. For four long months, nothing. Then the telegram arrived: Jean-Baptiste's oil tanker had been sunk by the Japanese in the Coral Sea; all aboard had perished.

Madame turned in my direction. "We received word of his

passing twenty-three years ago today. I hope he did not suffer too grievously. He was such a happy man and would have been a perfect father." She dabbed her eyes with a tissue. "We must do everything we can in this life. We are a long time dead."

DELIGHT: A momentary form of elation. I cannot say I have ever been a happy person, but I have certainly been able to take great pleasure in some things. Some books thrill me — so do many paintings and films. These fabrications overcome me with a momentary sense that everything is right with the world. Or that everything could be made right with the world. The illusion does not last long. Maybe that's why some people read all the time or frequent museums or see every movie they can? I guess there is within many of us a sanguine streak, one that survives despite all the obstacles thrown in the way.

DELUSIONS: Parents of most young children cannot believe their good fortune in having these wonderful gifts of life bestowed upon them. When youngsters reach adolescence, it is a different story — they insist on becoming their own masters. As a result, parents are often placed in turmoil.

Many are the nights Madame Beaulieu sat up waiting for one or more of her sons to cross the threshold. She worried about the usual things — girls getting pregnant, drugs, gangs — but her sons always remained dutiful. They would never have done anything to disgrace her, but each insisted on becoming his own person. Even someone as understanding as my landlady found this necessary process debilitating. When she could no longer idealize her offspring, she experienced a profound sense of disillusionment. Then, she decided that she had no real reason to feel disappointed or cheated.

Disillusionment, she taught herself, was the child of illusion. She often cautioned me about building fantasy castles in the air. "We all have imaginations, and we must use them. However, we cannot live our lives based on unrealistic expectations." This is one of the many valuable lessons Madame has imparted to me.

DEPARTED: When I was five, my closest friend was Émile, who was taller, more robust and much more talkative. In fact, he spoke so clearly, forcefully and intelligently that the nuns and priests held his intellect in high esteem. He was big-boned and somewhat ungainly, and these two factors made it difficult to "place" him in a good home, which he was determined to find.

The Robillards were not a childless couple. Bertrand was three when he accompanied his parents to the Orphanage. He was slight, scruffy and would not utter a word, not a single syllable. That is why the Robillards wanted to adopt: they were candid in stating that they wanted another child, who might inspire Bertrand — who had no physical disability of any kind — to speak. Under these circumstances, they determined to take Émile home with them.

The experiment worked. Within three months, the lazy vocal chords of Bertrand were a thing of the past, although for a long time Émile was the only person who could interpret his younger brother's speech.

Although Émile was happy in his new setting, he was jealous of his younger brother, who was clearly the favourite. He was not the type of boy to resort to kicking, punching or biting. He had a secretive side that allowed him to bide his time.

The family of four lived in the upper part of a duplex on de Maisonneuve Avenue in Montreal. Monsieur Robillard, a baker, was away every Sunday morning, and on that day his wife, who worked six days a week, had an insatiable craving to read. To satisfy this urge, she would walk three blocks to the newsagent who sold murder mystery magazines. At eight o'clock, she would set out alone on her quest, leaving Émile in charge of Bertrand. Once this pattern had been established, Émile went into action. He took some of his adopted mother's dearly beloved magazines and placed them on top of the gas stove and turned the burner on. Soon, the kitchen was filled with flames and smoke. After a few minutes — just as Madame Robillard returned home — he put out the flames and told his mother that Bertrand had performed that horrible deed while his back was turned.

The following Sunday, Madame Robillard, relentless in her pursuit of pulp fiction, tied Bertrand up with ropes and left him in his bedroom. As soon she left the house, Émile placed magazines on the burner, turned it on, waited a few minutes, and then untied his younger brother. As soon as she returned, Émile regaled his mother with a story of Bertrand's Houdini-like ability to untie knots and set a new fire.

On the third Sunday, Madame Robillard set out again, this time tying Bertrand even more securely to his bed. Émile again set a fire and, having looked out the window to be certain that his mother was on her way to the store, he began to untie his brother. He had not, however, reckoned sufficiently on the canniness of an adult familiar with gory stories. This time, the good lady doubled back and caught Émile in the midst of untying his captive brother.

A distraught Émile, certain that he had permanently blackened his copybook, was convinced that he would soon be on his way back to the Orphanage. He was startled when his adopted mother informed him that she understood exactly why he had undertaken his nefarious deed. "*Mon cher*, you think I don't love you enough. I shall try to be a better mother."

DIEFENBAKER, JOHN: I am glad that Mr. Pearson has replaced him as prime minister. For six long years — 1957 to 1963 — I was afraid of him. He has a very comical look — his huge jowls make him look like a demented hog — but he has a fierce temper. His energy is fuelled by pure anger. I knew he did not like French-Canadians, and I wondered if he would try to expel all of us from our native land.

DILETTANTE: A difficult word to spell, but an easy way of life. The amateur who never makes a commitment to become a professional. A person who settles for the would-be rather than the real.

The truth is that I fear that this is my assigned — or consigned — role in life. I am certain that I do not have the sufficient technical skills to be a genuine artist. Beyond that, do I know or feel enough so that the drawings that have been increasingly dominating my existence have any meaning beyond my humdrum existence? Who cares if Étienne draws secretly? The obvious answer is nobody. In the last year I have begun to care.

Yet I have no ambition to show my work; I do not wish it to be admired; I certainly do not want it to be subjected to critical gazes. It is something that has been forced on me. I think that makes me an amateur of the worst sort.

DONNELLY, MRS.: I wonder if she is still alive. I vividly recall the day I met her. I was eighteen and had just moved in with the Beaulieus. Seated regally behind her desk in the Young Peoples' Room at the Toronto Public Library, she was, as always, absorbed in a book. No other young person ever entered the room when I was there, and this experiment in attracting young adults must have been a dismal failure.

Mrs. Donnelly — she must have been in her fifties — had a plain elegance to her. Her blouses were always white, always topped by a single strand of pearls. Her cardigans and skirts were of the finest quality, often a soft grey in colour. Perhaps she felt this uniform was necessary for her to carry out her mission of seeking out converts to the pleasures of reading?

In those days, television was making sharp inroads — it was taking so many prisoners that the library was actively attempting to battle its pernicious influence. She knew I was what she often called a "kindred soul" when she referred to the poet John Donne. She informed me: "His name is not spelled as it is pronounced." I assured her that I was aware that it was D-O-N-N-E.

Her face was so warm and inviting that I approached the desk to ask her if she could recommend some books. Her delight in finding someone asking her to do her job was almost palpable.

Had I read Lucy Maud Montgomery? What about Sir Charles G.D. Roberts? She was unflustered when her eighteen-year-old visitor confessed to having devoured them all. What about Steinbeck, Hawthorne, Melville? The same responses did not intimidate her. Did I know *The Forsyte Saga*? When I confessed not to know anything about those books, her face lit up. She walked with me to the G section in fiction. "It's a bit adult in outlook, but you can handle it."

It took me five or six weeks to get through the adventures of Soames, Irene and the other bourgeois inhabitants of Galsworthy's fin de siècle world. Mrs. Donnelly's next recommendation was Pearl Buck's *The Good Earth*. "The book is exceptional in showing us a culture we know little about. Miss Buck went to China. She is one of the few Westerners who have any idea of what that country is really like."

For the next year, I eagerly followed her recommendations. One day, with a faraway look in her eyes, she told me: "You remind me of my son, Bobby. You even look a bit like him. The same dreamy look in the eyes. When he was your age, he was, like you, a voracious reader. They are the best kind."

One Saturday when I went to visit her, she was gone. The lady who had taken her place told me that Mrs. Donnelly's health had become so "precarious" that she had decided to retire.

DREAMS: I am tempted not to make an entry here but simply make a cross-reference to **NIGHTMARES**.

When I was tiny, five or six years old, I would be walking — transfixed with feelings of elation — with a kindly, attentive woman towards a rail station. I was looking forward to the journey we were about to take. Swiftly, we reached the station, where my caretaker would present our tickets and then usher me in the direction of the train. We would be about to mount the steps to our carriage. Suddenly, the train would take off. We would run after it to no avail. Then I would be completely alone, the station transformed into a field with grim, overhanging clouds. Then it would begin to rain. I would awake to discover that I had wet the bed.

As a young teenager, the dreams became even more terrifying. In one I was outside the Orphanage. For some reason I was filled with a sense of well-being. "Today will prove excellent," I told myself. The sun shone brightly; I ran carefree up and down the street. All of a sudden, I was aware that something special awaited me in one of the houses I was passing. I became tense because I could not stop and was sure that I was bypassing something of momentous importance. Despite my best efforts, I could not stop to investigate. I awoke from this nightmare in a cold sweat.

This dream had many variants. Sometimes I was able, with considerable effort, to stop myself so that I might explore the enticing house. Delighted, I looked around and saw a multiturreted mansion, a place of great beauty. Slowly, I walked towards it. The more I walked, the more distant the place became. I would awaken distraught.

There was an even more sinister version. I would finally manage to enter the enchanted house. The downstairs, appointed with the best furniture, contained not a single soul. Cautiously, I would make my way up the staircase and enter what was obviously the master bedroom. On the left-hand side of the bed rested a woman, her hands covering her face. Relieved to have discovered a fellow human being, I moved cautiously in her direction. She did not move. Finally, I announced my presence by calling to her. There was never any response. The woman on the bed never moved. From these dreams I would awaken in an anxiety-ridden state.

DROMEDARY: A romantic-sounding name for the one-humped camels; in scientific books this animal is properly called an even-toed ungulate. There are also the two-humped bactrians. By whatever names they are known, camels are often referred to as loutish, spitting, bad-tempered nuisances that despise their masters.

I have never been able to subscribe to this belief system. To me there is a majesty to them. They seem haughty as they look down upon us humans, and they are known to stamp their feet in displeasure. But I like the slow, angular steps they take through the dessert. Nature, by forcing them to conserve water within themselves, has provided us with a living metaphor of the careful use of the earth's resources.

In my drawings of camels, they are always at rest, sometimes sleeping, sometimes contemplating — their tiny eyes wide open — their fates. In my favourite picture, a camel lies before the viewer with its head twisting sinuously backwards and resting on its reservoir of water. Ears flapped backwards, eyes staring straight ahead, he accepts his fate as a wanderer on the hostile sands of the Sahara.

DUPLESSIS, MAURICE: The father of modern Quebec, many say. He is despised in Ontario because of the financial demands he made upon the federal government, which considered him a kind of swashbuckling pirate. In Ontario he was seen as the embodiment of what it is to be a "frog": Catholic, family centred, corrupt, freeloading and lazy.

Many people in Quebec have come to despise Duplessis, who passed away almost ten years ago. Last year, in 1966, Madame Beaulieu told me that she had heard from a reliable source that he had taken many small children out of orphanages and placed them in mental asylums. When I asked her why he would do such a preposterous thing, she informed me that he could obtain a great deal more federal money for a lunatic than for a found-ling. Therefore, he insisted on the change of address of hundreds of poor children, many of whom might be incarcerated for the remainder of their lives.

E, more than any other letter, attracts the colour green. Wonderful greens. Deep-purple-tinged greens. Pale yellow-infused shades of the colour. There is no more soothing letter. I am glad that it is the most frequent of them all.

THE ED SULLIVAN SHOW: As far as television is concerned, no one in the Beaulieu home is a nationalist. We do not watch Juliette or Tommy Hunter. More than Sunday Mass, which we all attend regularly, The Ed Sullivan Show on Sunday nights is the staple of our lives in the Beaulieu household.

Madame Beaulieu insists the phone be ignored if anyone is foolish enough to ring between eight and nine p.m. In fact, she becomes incensed at the basic ignorance of anyone foolish enough to miss this great TV entertainment.

The mournful little sparrow, Edith Piaf, is Madame's all-time favourite of Ed's guests. "Such feeling she transmits from her tiny, bony body," she once observed, tears falling down her face. "I think she smokes too much," Madame added maternally. Frank, winking at me, suggested Piaf might also be too partial to whisky and heroin. His wife promptly shushed him. When Piaf died four years ago, Madame dressed in black for two weeks.

Madame became incensed with her husband when he confessed that he enjoyed the pulsating rhythms of The Supremes, but she was apoplectic when her sons informed her The Rolling Stones were the best act ever to grace the Sullivan show. I put myself on safer ground when I offered the opinion that the appearance of The Beatles on February 4, 1964 was my most treasured memory. Madame bowed in my direction: "I like their music, but I do not like mophead haircuts."

Just as the show is about to begin, Madame often observes, "Ed is a very nice man. He loves everybody who visits him. He is the perfect host. Tonight will be another BEEEG show."

THE EDGE OF NIGHT: Madame Beaulieu is very embarrassed if anyone in our household refers to this serial, which she compulsively watches every weekday afternoon. She is infatuated with lawyer Mike Karr, his wife Sara and the city of Monticello where they live. Unlike *As the World Turns* — which specializes in love affairs and which Madame Beaulieu views as a show beneath contempt — Monticello is an ordinary-looking American city that just happens to be filled with gangsters, drug dealers, blackmailers, kidnapper, spies and corrupt politicians.

She has a penchant for the steamy side of the States. "I do not smoke; I do not drink. I have to have one vice." This is my landlady's defence if her husband, one of her sons or I poke fun at this addiction.

EMMANUEL: Another name for the Christ Child. For me, it refers to the newborn protagonist in Marie-Claire Blais' *Une Saison dans la vie d' Emmanuel*, published in 1965. The baby, the sixteenth child of poverty-stricken farmers in Quebec, is a very observant, sometimes wary toddler. Emmanuel's mother, who has to work, cannot attend to him and so he is given into the care of his grouchy but often tender grandmother. From her he learns that life is mainly a series of miseries interrupted by explosive moments of joy. At the very end of the narrative, the child discovers a form of salvation: "Emmanuel wasn't cold anymore. The sun was shining on the land. A tranquil warmth was flowing through his veins as his grandmother rocked him in her arms. Emmanuel was emerging from the dark."

Where did life lead Emmanuel? My suspicion is that he seized the day, abandoned his rural existence, emigrated to Montreal and became an artist.

ENEMIES: The last person I hoped to see after I left the Orphanage was Fred. Every so often I espied someone in the street who resembled him and was grateful each time that it was not. I was flabbergasted when he arrived at the Beaulieus late one Sunday afternoon six years ago in 1960. He rang the door-bell and was invited in by Madame, who then went up and knocked at my door: "An old friend has dropped in to see you."

Fred was beaming when I walked into the living room and shook his hand. "I haven't seen you in over ten years," he proclaimed, as if this was an unexpected and unfortunate turn of events. He had run into another former inmate who knew where I lived. The implication was that he was taking the initiative in renewing an old intimacy. Madame B left the room, whereupon Fred began to reminisce about our former lives. Waves of nostalgia flooded him. For him, these were the good old days.

Fifteen years before, Fred had been the ringleader of all bullying at the Orphanage. I had been his chief victim. In those days, I often began sentences by qualifying them: "I think" or "I hope." He would respond: "Something is so or it ain't so, fancy pants."

I have always been a daydreamer lost in my own little world. Fred attacked me mercilessly for that. He also observed that I had what he considered a mechanical way of speaking, as if a robot were talking. "I think this guy's not all there," he would mockingly inform his subordinates.

These were the least of his offences. When I was eleven or twelve, he would routinely knock me down for the amusement of his entourage. When we got older, he directed obscene gestures my way, the chief of which was to move his right hand as if masturbating. "I bet you don't know how to play with yourself. Want me to teach you?" When Fred left the Orphanage, he simply vanished. I had no interest in finding out where he had gone.

Now, here in the Beaulieus' living room, he was acting as if we had been the best of pals. Fred was very solicitous about my welfare. He had some nondescript job involving scrap metal.

Once very stocky, he was now what I would call slim. His deep-olive skin still had masses of eruptions; his hooded eyes remained observant yet wary. After speaking at me for about an hour, he asked if he could take me out to dinner some night. I mumbled some half-hearted words of agreement.

That night was filled with nightmares, all of which involved Fred as Torturer and me as Victim. After that, Fred telephoned several times and left messages for me with Madame Beaulieu. I never responded.

Why, after all these years, had Fred decided to get in touch with me? Why would he want to see me? At first, I thought he wanted to renew our relationship at a new, adult level. On reflection, I doubt this is correct.

Even as a child, there might have been something about me that he liked or admired. He couldn't face up to that and so became my tormenter. As an adult, he might have been able to put the past into perspective and so hope to forge a new kind of relationship. Of course, the simplest — and probably correct — answer is that he felt guilty about what he had done and wanted to make amends.

ETHEL MERTZ: I love Lucy, but I have a soft spot for her side-kick, Ethel Mertz. Red-haired, big-mouthed Lucy is a screwball, pure and simple. Ethel is a much more cunning person, someone with a ruthless side. Hands on hips, modestly dressed, hair tightly curled, she swaggers whereas Lucy flounces. Ethel has what Madame Beaulieu once claimed to be "a lot of moxie." She is always interested in how much money she might make out of one of Lucy's schemes. A victim of her marriage to the miserly Fred, she is openly contemptuous of her husband whereas Lucy claims to idealize Ricky.

Lucy may shoot the spitballs, but Ethel manufactures them. I do not think quickly on my feet — I also am not prone to the catchy phrase or the witty comeback. I am much more like ham-fisted Lucy than quick-witted Ethel.

When belittled at work, I vent my feelings only to myself. I live in envy of people like Ethel who have the courage to tell their enemies exactly what they think of them.

EXOTIC: Something I know little about from first-hand experience. Never having travelled anywhere until I went to China almost ten years ago, I am in some ways not the ideal person to read books set in faraway lands. In fact, as a child, the only stories I read about faraway places were the black-and-white Tintin books (*Tintin au Congo*, *Les Cigares du Pharaon*, *Le Lotus bleu*) that one of the nuns — born in Belgium — had loaned to us. These narratives — because they were written in French — were not regarded by the authorities as trashy comic books.

As a ten- and eleven-year-old, I was given the nickname of Hergé's hero because, like Tintin, I have a reddish tinge to my hair and a stand-up lick of it that refuses to be combed down. At that time, I imagined myself, accompanied by Snowy (*Milou* in French), Tintin's white Fox Terrier, engaged in all sorts of spectacular escapades in a variety of foreign places.

I suspect that the occupants of the Orphanage liked Tintin in large part because he was terribly young and had no parents. We could well identify with his difficulties in dealing with an uncertain world.

EYE: For artists, there is an intimate connection between the letter I and the word *eye*. Without the latter, the former cannot exist.

F is the Hamlet of the alphabet. Very indecisive. It is forced to ask itself on a daily basis, Am I just some sort of bedraggled E? It only finds its individuality when its smaller horizontal line is elaborately embellished.

There are many other difficulties, the most prominent of which is the F-word. F would do almost anything in its power to rid itself of that encumbrance.

FAKING: I study books on art in order to see things that I can "adapt" in my drawings. At the Toronto Public Library, some of the librarians will call my attention to a new book. "You might want to look at this biography of Dürer," a very pleasant young woman informed me the other day as she put the book in my hands. She and her colleagues have no idea that I am a would-be artist. They think I am simply an admirer, which of course I am. I scour widely: Mt. Fuji by Hokusai, Venetian street scenes by Canaletto, anything that will give me an idea. My borrowing from other artists has never given me much pause — after all, every good artist steals from his predecessors. I had no doubts about the rightness of my actions until yesterday, when the manager asked me if I could leave work an hour early and take some papers to Cedric Smith for his signature. Mr. Smith has not been well lately, and several certificates are up for renewal.

Mr. Smith may be a man of considerable means, but he lives alone in a narrow, dishevelled house on Baldwin Street. I have often walked by his residence and noticed the vast accumulation of weeds in what should be a front garden and the many layers of paint peeling from the front door.

A gentleman of the old school, Mr. Smith received me warmly and invited me to take a glass of sherry. According to the records at the Bank, he is 78, but he looks much older. He stoops badly, his thick white mane of hair is matted and his face is beet red. He nodded in the direction of his sitting room and told me to take a seat while he fetched our drinks.

That room is long and stretches back a great distance. The stuffed furniture was once expensive but is now tattered. I could not make much headway in assessing the room because my eyes were drawn to the paintings that occupied all the wall space. A large Constable, a medium-sized Van Gogh, a tiny Rembrandt and many other treasures.

"I see that you are studying my collection, Étienne," the old man observed as he entered the room.

"Yes, sir. It is very impressive." I decided not to say more.

"You may not be aware of it, my dear boy, but all these canvases can be seen at the Art Gallery of Ontario."

"Indeed. I have been to the museum many times, and I recognize many old friends."

"Good for you. I thought you might be a person of culture and have a shock of recognition. This has been my avocation: making copies of paintings."

Chuckling to himself, he went on: "If you look carefully, you will see little difference between my Constable and the Constable on public display. I never seek to 'improve' the work of others but to replicate them faithfully."

"I can see that. You have remarkable skill."

"Your compliment is much appreciated. I have learned a great deal from my hobby. Art is simply the art of mechanical reproduction. Nothing more. I have now concluded my experiments and know, as I long suspected, that artists are really artisans."

This remark was made with some malice, as if he had conducted a battle with the likes of Raphael and El Greco and emerged the winner. I did not dare ask him about inspiration, about the fact that the inspiration for the paintings had come from the tortured souls of their creators.

FILMS: Ever since I moved in with the Beaulieus and obtained my first job, I have treated myself to a film every week, almost always on Saturday evenings. I love the secrecy of cinemas. First there is the total annihilation of light. Then there is a slight whir of sound from the projector followed by a thin stream of light aimed at and penetrating the white screen. Then the magic enfolds.

As a young adult, I must admit that my taste was at best plebian. My gods and goddesses were the likes of Tony Curtis, Piper Laurie and the Vancouver-born Yvonne DeCarlo. I was captivated by colour films set in the Middle East. *Son of Ali Baba* was my favourite. Caliphs, fakirs, thieves, princesses, magic carpets and secret caves. This was the world into which I yearned to escape. I would settle for a Western, but it was not a genre that captured my imagination. *Tarzan* and other jungle films were fine, but I loathed science fiction.

When I was seven years old, all of the orphans were taken on an outing to see a film about flying saucers. All day I imagined a comic fantasy adventure about porcelain pieces flying in space. The reality that evening — a sinister film about alien invaders — gave me bad dreams for weeks afterwards.

FLAG: Thanks to Mr. Pearson, Canada received a flag two years ago in 1965, just in the nick of time for the one hundredth anniversary of Confederation: it is referred to as the Maple Leaf — in Quebec, *l'Unifolié*. It is a simple red flag with a white square in its centre featuring an eleven-pointed maple leaf. It's a simple-enough design, but the mayhem surrounding its choice was disgusting. In essence, Pearson's opponents wanted a form of the Union Jack — the so-called "Red Ensign" or "Red Duster" — so that the dominance of the English over the French was permanently enshrined. Another example of how the French-Canadian is made to feel a castaway.

FLAMINGOS: What omniscient being could create such a beautiful, ridiculous-looking creature with his long neck, small head, high-pitched *chissick* and slow, *murr*-ing bleat? The deep rose-pink variety are called "Lesser Flamingos" by ornithologists, whereas the completely white, larger ones are dubbed "Greater Flamingos." Surely the Lesser are really the Greater?

FOO DOGS: Since my visit to China, I remain entranced by these stone creatures, completely mythological beings. Large examples guard important buildings. Tiny ones can be found in all the colours of jade.

No dog ever looked quite so much a lion. They may give themselves the air of ferocity, but they are so puffed up with self-importance that they give themselves away. Their grimaces are a bold lie: they are quintessentially domestic animals.

At a stall in Shanghai I noticed a small jade sculpture of two of these dogs fighting. Although carved from a single piece of stone, the animal on top was dark grey (almost black) whereas his opponent was a dull, musty white. The carver made perfect use of his material. The dark animal occupied about two thirds of the piece, and the white one — in the process of being bested — had to settle for the remaining space. The countenances of both animals were determined, but I could detect arrogance in the smirk on the face of the victor whereas his opponent looked as if he realized he might — despite his best efforts — be destroyed.

That day I was forced to ask myself, was the artist commenting on the dominance of evil in the modern world, or did he simply have to make the best use of the small piece of stone with which he had been entrusted? If the stone had been two-thirds white, would he have shown the triumph of goodness?

FOOTBALL: Not a sport to which French-Canadians are drawn. Frank Beaulieu — who likes a tall tale as much as I do — once told me the story of the mayor of Montreal who was invited to the Grey Cup festivities in which Toronto played Montreal for the championship of the Canadian Football League. This man spoke little English and had no interest in football. Called upon to speak, he decided to make a virtue of brevity. Summoning the little English he possessed, he proclaimed, "I am glad to kick off your ball today and in the future I hope to kick off all your balls!"

FOREIGN FILMS: No one at the Bank will go to a subtitled film under any circumstances. I suspect this is a form of xenophobia. At first I was deeply suspicious of people like Fellini and Antonioni. I must admit I found the films of Resnais pretentious.

Then a truth dawned. These people had a completely different take on the world from Hollywood. Films did not have to have endings in which everything was wrapped up neatly; they did not have to reach happy conclusions; they could be about ordinary things without convoluted twists and turns.

FORTY-SIX YONGE STREET: This building on the southwest corner of Yonge and Wellington streets has had, like every human being I know, its share of ups and downs.

That modest-looking building began life as a hotel, then it became the emporium of J.G. Joseph, the city's finest jeweller and silversmith in the 1860s and 1870s, then it became the head office of the now defunct Standard Bank, then of the Trader's Bank (also defunct), and, presently, it is a store called National

Wholesale, which proudly announces, "Selling Directly to the Public."

We are all in flux — our lives but mere grains of sand in a vast desert.

FRAGILE: Over the years I have overheard some of my fellow employees apply this word to me. I think that they mean I am overly sensitive to criticism. I do take recriminations — no matter how kindly meant — to heart. I know this and struggle with it, sometimes to no avail. Often tears well up. Or my face turns beet red. "You could try to deal with customers more quickly," is one complaint. "You are not a good salesman of Canada Bonds. You have to be more aggressive. Tell customers it is their patriotic duty to buy them."

"Steve has no social life outside the Bank," is another loudly whispered observation. My feelings are hurt. I do not like people to make this comment about me. On the other hand, the statement is true. I am a loner. I am afraid of crowds.

I did notice that the word "SCHIZOID" was written underneath OCD on my doctor's file. Of course, I also looked up that word. Schizoids are people who avoid the company of others. They prefer not to be connected to others. This sickness is a difficult one to treat because such persons do not place any value on attachment.

FRAUD: At the Bank we have to make sure that we do not accept counterfeit money. We are vigilantly anti-fraud.

After my encounter with Mr. Smith the other day, I have come to the opinion that he is a complete fraud. Somehow or other, he thinks that he can pilfer the soul of a Rembrandt and put it on canvas. His mechanics may be excellent, but he is devoid of inspiration. Does he have any idea that people visit museums in order to worship the creative spirit?

FRENCH-CANADIANS: Sounds like a neutral enough term. Not like using the racist words *kike* to describe a Jewish person or *nigger* to refer to a Negro. Yet, the word, when used by English-Canadians, has several subsidiary meanings:

a. draft dodger — someone not willing to fight to defend Canada;
b. a member of the underclass;
c. someone who cannot speak proper English;
d. someone who prefers the benefits of unemployment insurance to a regular job;
e. the likely ethnicity of any culprit in an armed robbery.

FRIENDS: This is a concept that eludes me. Every Thursday I would purchase the weekly comic to read eagerly of the adventures of Archie, Betty, Veronica, Jughead and Reggie. They were fun-loving, stupid teenagers: Archie loved Veronica, who spurned him; Betty was hopelessly in love with Archie, who spurned her; Jughead was a loveable jerk; the handsome Reggie was the foil to ordinary looking, accident-prone Archie. Geraldine Grundy was the English teacher who found fault with these youngsters. There were many other characters. In this universe, despite many trials and tribulations, Archie and his gang always prevailed. I used to read those comics because in them I found solace and could imagine myself as one of their hangers-on, as someone who could freely enter their world. They were my imaginary friends.

I have often heard fellow employees whisper behind my back, "He has no friends. He has no social life." In the main, that is absolutely true. Over the years I have not kept in touch with my fellow inmates from the Orphanage in Toronto. Occasionally, I encounter one of them. Virginie, for example.

The circumstances of her early life are similar to my own. About five months after I was found, she was discovered in a trash can a few blocks from the Hôtel Dieu. She almost died, so extreme was the hypothermia to which she had been subjected. I can remember her at about the age of five, her head crowned with thick black curls, her eyes a sapphire blue. According to the nuns, such a charming young girl should have had no trouble attracting a good home. When prospective parents visited and asked to be introduced to her, she would exchange her usually placid demeanour for that of a wildcat. She threatened to bite or scratch any visitor who approached her and so she was never adopted. One day she made a strange confession to me. She felt guilty not only that her mother had abandoned her but that she could not remember what she looked like.

"You were only a few hours old when she discarded you."

"Yes, but if I had kept my eyes open in the womb — or had opened them at birth — I would now be able to recall what she looked like. That would comfort me."

Like me, she was very bright at school. Unlike me, her ability to obtain top marks never deserted her. In fact, she became better with age. I left the Orphanage two years before her, but I later learned that she had attended Jarvis Collegiate for Grade Thirteen and won an all-expenses scholarship to the University of Toronto.

Ten years ago, I encountered Virginie on Harbord Street. "Is that you, Tintin?" The young woman asking the question had a straight, black, pageboy haircut.

"Yes. It's me. I don't remember you."

"Trust you not to recognize an old friend," she responded in French.

It took me a moment or two before the past came into focus. "I haven't seen you in a long time, Virginie."

"My name's Ginnie," she informed me. "Are you at U of T?"

"No. I work at the Bank over there."

"You're a teller?"

I nodded.

"What a waste," she exclaimed. "You're too smart for that."

"Sometimes I think so, but it is the only job I could get."

"At least it's gainful employment." She then went on to tell me that she was in third-year ELL. When I told her that I did not know what that meant, she informed me that she was in English Language and Literature. She liked studying literature, although she had no idea what she would do with it in the future. "Grad school maybe," she added.

I ran into her a year later at almost the same spot. She informed me that she had a wonderful boyfriend — a Ph.D. candidate specializing in Wordsworth — and was marrying him the following month. "I'm preggers," she proudly added.

Three years after that, I saw Ginnie near Yonge and Bloor. Her clothes looked like she had costumed herself in a bunch of rags. The little boy holding her hand was well-dressed. In fact, he looked happy. Ginnie's attention seemed divided between the child and looking forlornly behind her, as if on guard lest an avenging angel overtake and slay them.

I hesitated, but I decided to cross the street to speak with her. "Hi Ginnie." She looked me full in the face, but no recognition glimmered. She walked on as if I had not spoken. The boy looked curiously in my direction.

Years later, I read in the *Telegraph* that Ginnie had married, but her husband had abandoned her and the boy. She had kept the child, but Children's Aid removed him from her when he was about three years old. She was an unfit mother because she had become a heavy drinker. About a year after that, she threw herself from the Bloor Street Viaduct.

G

G is as wide as it is high and is a figure of monumental, enclosed heaviness that can only be relieved when attention is paid to the curve of its base or when its horizontal line is either made completely simple or imaginatively decorated. G's lot is a troublesome one: it is fretful letter that, as it were, must be handled with kid gloves.

G also has a complex character. Bach wrote his *Air on a G String* so that the violin solo fits entirely on the lowest of the violin's four strings. That sounds very chaste and otherworldly, but **G-Men** are stern, gun-toting officers of the law. And the letter has a naughty side. The women at the Victory Burlesque on Spadina (I have been there once) cavort in **G-strings**.

GARRULOUS: An adjective that could never be applied to me. That is one so-called defect I would not mind possessing.

As a child and teenager I was the despair of any priest who listened to my confession. I would bless myself, admit that I had sinned, state how long since my last confession, and then become silent.

"Well, what do you wish to own up to?" the priest would inquire.

I realized, for instance, that I had been silently angry at a fellow inmate and should mention this failing. Somehow or other, I could not put the words together.

"Are you telling me that you have done nothing wrong, not committed the slightest infraction, have no venial sins to tell me about?"

Silence.

"Étienne, I noticed that you had a spat with Genevieve the other day. Is that not true?"

After I admitted to that, further questions would follow. When I became older, my various confessors were sure that I did not own up to having impure thoughts. Or to having performed impure acts. They interrogated me: "Have you touched yourself?" I would then be reminded that this was a mortal sin which, if I did not share this information and repent the act, could lead me to be cast into the fires of hell.

The inability to speak was followed by the unwillingness to speak. Why should I tell these men any secrets I possessed? As a young teenager, I became convinced that I was a true villain worthy of God's most severe retribution.

GOOSEBUMPS: I would often get these as a child when I stepped out of the bath. Nowadays, if I come upon a particularly beautiful painting, drawing, sculpture or poem they assail me. Much more pleasant sensation than that other childhood affliction, hiccups.

GORGEOUS GEORGE: Madame Beaulieu is a very tolerant person, but, unfortunately, she dislikes both Milton Berle and Jack Benny. The former is simply "silly" and the latter a "cheapskate." The wrestler is another matter.

Glaring at her husband and me, her hands on her hips, she raises her voice: "Why you two would waste your time looking at that fake, I have no idea!" She may dislike his platinum-blond hair, his gold-plated bobby pins, his sequined dressing gown and his entrance to the strains of *Pomp and Circumstance*, but she is even more annoyed by his valet Jeffries, who carries a silver-plated mirror and spreads rose petals at his master's feet. She does not like the fact that the servant sprays the "Human Orchid" with Chanel No. 5. She certainly does not wish her sons — whom she forces to leave the room with her when the show begins — to be corrupted by the great man's often-repeated outcry, "Win if you can, lose if you must, but always cheat!"

Frank smiles at me during his wife's outbursts. Like me, he knows that George is a great comic actor, a man who has constructed himself in the service of television. When George lost to Whipper Billy Watson at Maple Leaf Gardens in March 1959 and had his golden locks shaved bald, Madame Beaulieu conducted herself as a Delilah who had finally tamed her Samson.

GOULD, GLENN: Like me, a misfit. Three years ago the pianist renounced the concert stage, supposedly to concentrate on making "perfect" recordings.

For him, the world is contaminated. Best not to wander too far from home. In your own space, you can wash your hands as often as you please.

GREAT EXPECTATIONS: Whenever anyone at the Bank learns that I am an orphan, they almost invariably respond: "I know how awful that experience must be. I read *Great Expectations* in high school." I nod sagely in their direction.

The truth is I dislike Pip intensely and do not wish anyone to impose his identity upon me. For one thing, Pip is a self-absorbed person. His sister's husband, Joe, bestows plenty of affection on him, but that is not good enough for Pip, who becomes a consummate snob certain that the loathsome Miss Havisham is his guardian angel. We all suffer from self-delusions, but Pip cultivates and embraces his.

GREEN: Whenever I tell people that green is my favourite colour, they inform me I have made a bad choice. "Blue is far safer, more universal," someone told me point blank. "Green comes from blue."

There are also a great many proponents of red. These people tend to lose their tempers easily. (I would never choose red because, like Anne of Green Gables, I am very self-conscious about having red hair, although nowadays the carrot-red has given way to what I can euphemistically call strawberry-blond.) "Green is the colour associated with jealousy," another person remarked. "You're not Irish," I have also been informed.

Forest green, lime green, cactus green, olive green, avocado green, pear green, iceberg lettuce green, chartreuse, lawn green, broccoli green, algae green, emerald green, bottle green, shamrock green, cucumber green. I suppose each colour has its own infinite variety, but these fill me with a feeling of hope — that nature is constantly in the process of renewing itself.

I'm well aware that people whisper behind my back that I'm completely green. "He's not an adult, has never grown up. Can't figure out what's wrong with him."

Some people have attempted to rid me of one kind of greenness. The most dedicated person was Marguerite-Anne Darling from Syracuse, New York. When I worked at the Royal Bank branch near her apartment in the Annex, she made a point of always coming to my wicket. She soon told me that she was in fourth-year honours Art History at the University of Toronto and had been away from school for a few years because of "personal problems." A few months after we first met, she would regularly wait for me outside the Bank and ask me to drop by for coffee.

In contrast to me, Marguerite-Anne — who became incensed if anyone mistakenly called her *Margaret-Anne*, or dropped the *Anne*, or, in a note or letter dropped the *e* in *Anne* — had a lot to say. I suppose we became boon companions because she talked rapidly while I listened attentively.

It did not take me long to notice that Marguerite-Anne was obsessed with various kinds of boyfriends: "boys-next-door," "studs," "fraternity animals," and "dreamboats" were often-used expressions. There was also a special category of "weird" types:

these were young men who were unusual-looking or -acting. They were quite acceptable as long as they "got down to business." After a while, I realized that indiscreet hints were being thrown in my direction. According to her, I was "weird" but could become "acceptable" if I "got down to business."

I was not the slightest bit interested in Marguerite-Anne. She had a lantern jaw, scraggly, greasy, red hair and bit-chewed fingernails. I do not know if she owned a dress; she was always attired in dungarees, as if she were a labourer in some farmer's fields. I was given more than a hint of her intentions towards me when she handed me some business cards she had just obtained — these gave her name, telephone number and a quotation: "It's a business doing pleasure with you." I pretended not to know what this statement meant.

She is the person who dragged me to the Victory, obviously hoping to get me in a romantic mood. I did not enjoy myself — I was offended by the sight of the woman, dressed in the habit of a nun, who raucously removed her wimple, headgear and clothing and then caressed her breasts and G-string-covered private parts with her rosary beads.

When we were coming out of that theatre, she nudged me and whispered, "Under those suits of yours, you have a nice body. Perhaps you should think about using it." Then she gave me what she thought was a Marlene Dietrich sneer.

I did not know how to extricate myself from this would-be virago. The next time we met for coffee, she told me in elaborate detail about a transatlantic crossing she had made the year before. On the way to Europe, there were a number of body builders who were to compete for the title of Mr. Universe in

Rome. According to her, she "sampled" each of them. On her way back, she had encountered a transvestite, with whom she formed a close friendship. On the final night at sea, the Captain was holding a ball. Jean had an evening dress designed by Worth — "blue and sparkly" — and intended to appear as Jeanne if Marguerite-Anne would consent to appear as Marvin. My friend readily agreed to this proposal, costumed herself in a tuxedo provided by Jean and they danced the night away.

For a long time I had become convinced that Marguerite-Anne was a consummate liar. I still do not understand what got into me that afternoon, but I accused her of being mendacious. She looked me steadily and steely in the eye, stood up and started to rummage in her filing cabinet. A few minutes later, she smiled, handed me a large manila envelope and ordered me to open it. Inside were a series of black and white photographs — each five by seven inches — obviously taken aboard ship in which a demure Jeanne with a prominent five o'clock shadow stood next to Marvin: Marguerite-Anne smiled benignly into the camera, enfolding her beloved.

That afternoon, after I apologized, Marguerite-Anne discoursed about a wide variety of topics. We took our leave after an hour. A few days later, I handled the paperwork from central branch that transferred her account to another bank. I never saw her again. I was obviously much too green, even for her.

GROUP OF SEVEN: I feel disloyal to my French-Canadian heritage by stating how much I like the experimental do-and-dare of this English-Canadian 1920s coterie — really a Group of Eleven if one is interested in accuracy. These men looked at all the stale Victorian-inspired landscapes that constituted Canadian landscape painting, declared them rubbish, went to the northern part of Ontario to look at the primitive land there and then fashioned a painting style that was based partly on observation, partly on the newer trends in European art.

The landscapes I draw are so much my "take" on what I have observed that I readily sympathize with what these men were trying to do: find the essence of trees, water and mountains. Do spirits live in these inanimate objects? I hope there are some inhabiting my puny efforts.

H

H is a model of simplicity and integrity. Its fence-like structure prevents it from having any pretence to handsomeness. The crossbar dividing its two verticals must be rendered expressively for it to have any hope of catching the eye. If a letter can be said to be a wallflower, that claim can be made for H. I often think myself its human equivalent.

For the native French speaker, H is a landmine. As a young child, it was drilled into me that I had to learn to pronounce this troublesome letter correctly. I had to memorize when to drop it, when to pronounce it. Madame Beaulieu finds H very pesky. For example, she always refers to *tunderstorms* and then smiles embarrassedly if she is speaking with the letter carrier or a neighbour.

HASSELBLAD: The ultimate in brand-name luxury. When I was unexpectedly given two hundred dollars, I felt a hole burning in my pocket. I wandered down to the camera stores on the seedy parts of Yonge Street. A strange fantasy overtook me. Perhaps I should take photographs in Shanghai, which I was being forced to visit. I dismissed the idea as preposterous. Then the monster of pride — as I labelled it that day — overcame me. Why shouldn't I treat myself and use the windfall to buy a really good camera? A part of me whispered, Am I an artist-in-waiting after all?

I was aghast at the feelings that were attempting to exert themselves. I wanted to disown them. In a state of indecision, I wandered into a store and beheld a Hasselblad 500c. The sight of this marvel of Swedish design, with its elegant, grey, leather-covered boxlike structure — mesmerized me. The top popped open to allow the user to gaze down on an especially large viewing area. If I had control of that instrument, my powers of invention might well be released, I told myself. In that moment of indecisiveness and greed, I handed over the money I had received two hours before.

HEPBURN: Strange that Audrey and Katharine share the same surname. Whenever I see waiflike, doe-eyed Audrey, I am certain that my mother looks likes her. For days afterwards, I imagine this child-woman, costumed as in *The Nun's Story*, attending to my every need. Heavy-jawed Katharine is both witty and irascible — and inordinately self-centred. I would have to look after her.

HERO: A boy without mother or father is the ideal hero in any work of fiction because he is free in the way those living in families can never be. He should be able to chart his own life and thus master his own destiny. In this instance, fiction bears little resemblance to lived experience.

I remain drawn to the exploits of the Lone Ranger, Hopalong Cassidy, and Superman. When I behold how dexterously they handle all the difficulties put in their way, I can imagine myself confronting such obstacles with equal magnificence. But, as soon as one of the TV episodes is over, I feel cheated: I will never have to worry about rustlers stealing cattle. How are these men helping me live my humdrum existence?

HIDE-AND-SEEK: Endless hours at the Orphanage playing this game. For us, it was a wonderful pastime. You search for someone lost and, whether you win or not, the missing person is restored. For persons of my background, this is a comforting activity.

HIEROGLYPH: As a student of the alphabet, I have a deep-seated love for the ancient Egyptians and their picture-words. Whenever I go to the Royal Ontario Museum, I make a point of descending to the basement to look at the sarcophagus on which all that mystical writing is embellished. Those glyphs — each embedded with picture, sound and language — display the greatness of the human mind.

HIPPOPOTAMUS: A wonderful word for those large, lumbering, thick-skinned beasts. I imagine they endure incredibly arduous winters in Parkdale at the zoo. I often think of the poor beast slain in ancient Rome.

HIROSHIMA MON AMOUR: I was thirteen at the time the bombs descended on Hiroshima and Nagasaki. There was much rejoicing here in Canada — the war would finally be over. Then a week later we began to see the newsreels showing the devastation. People, many of them children — some badly maimed — wandered over the terrain of what had been their homes. Children of my age, their skin and clothing charred, had become zombies. A month or two later, there were further reports: the faces of the victims were badly pitted, their backs and limbs tattooed with horrifying landscapes. A year after that came the footage showing newborns, some with missing legs or arms.

That is my Hiroshima. Then there is the film in which, during World War II, a teenage Frenchwoman from Nevers has an affair with a German soldier. He is shot dead by locals, and she has her hair shorn to commemorate her disgrace. Many years later in Japan she encounters a Japanese architect, whose family perished at Hiroshima, and sleeps with him. For her, he becomes the dead German soldier — the past becomes the present. All of this is told against the backdrop of Hiroshima, much of the footage from the past inserted into the narrative by the director, Alain Resnais.

"You are destroying me," the woman tells her lover. "I cannot live without you," she quickly adds.

The film is constructed of paradox after paradox. The woman will always be in Nevers; the architect will always be in Hiroshima. The past can never be erased. As I watched the film and beheld the sad early life of the woman, I could not help thinking that my birth might have had a similar traumatic effect on my mother's existence.

Against my will, I imagined that my real mother bore a striking likeness to Emmanuelle Riva, whose beautiful face was the embodiment of grief. She may have physically survived the war, but she would always be emotionally dead. I began to grieve for the woman who had given me life, although I realized that even if I were to encounter her, I could do little to assist her. She would remain beyond my ability to redeem her.

HOCKEY: According to Mr. Beaulieu and his three sons, Canada's true heroes are its hockey players — rough, badly groomed, devil-may-care. The four are rabid supporters of the Canadiens, but that loyalty is sometimes called into question when they witness the exploits of one of the great Quebec-born players on the Toronto Maple Leafs or the American teams — Detroit, Boston, New York and Chicago.

Beyond question in the minds of the Beaulieus is that the French-Canadian male demonstrates week after week his superiority at Canada's national game.

There are some lively paradoxes at work in this belief system. Canada's national game is really Quebec's. If this is so, where does this leave the whole idea of national unity? Very much in the dust, as far as Mr. Beaulieu is concerned.

The French-Canadian player is resolute, indefatigable, persevering, and canny. Of course, these are the very traits that the Anglos claim that the French lack in the business world. For Mr. Beaulieu, the actions of these athletes prove not only the superior physical strength of Quebecers but also their high overall accomplishments.

I learned to skate when I was five or six. I have always been an indifferent skater but, strangely, a more than adequate goalie. "Étienne has a sixth-sense of where the puck is going to land," one coach remarked. "That kid really knows how the spread himself around so that the puck can't get by him," another claimed. Despite my early glory days in the sport, I have never enjoyed *Hockey Night in Canada* and am glad to escape to the movies every Saturday night in winter while poor Madame B stoically sits through that evening's television.

HOLY OFFICE: The nuns referred to this entity reverentially. As a young child, I could not understand the expression. I imagined a small room hidden away in the Vatican where a group of saints chatted with each other while incense wafted in the air. As an adult, one may abandon Church doctrine, but the scent of that heady perfume remains comforting.

HUMMINGBIRDS: In the spring and summer, on the way to work, I see the occasional one — usually a florescent green — having its way with a purple cone flower. They do not fly; they zigzag. They attack life vigorously, draining its essence. Where do these miniscule animals originate? If tiny pieces of rubies and sapphires were given leave to abandon their mineral states, they would become hummingbirds. Matter-of-factly, Darwin would label this speculation nonsensical.

I

I is the letter of loneliness, standing completely on its own. It possesses its own special bravery as it stands naked and terribly exposed before the complex strokes that make up its brothers and sisters. Such a small sign to bear the weight of our enormous egos.

ILLUMINATION: If we did but know it, every person and every thing in the universe is decorated in the wondrous colours of nature.

I learned this wonderful lesson when Sister Magdalena suggested I study medieval illumination. In fact, she showed me some modern reproductions of such books. At what I suspect was a considerable expense she purchased gouache paint, coloured inks, the gum ammoniac used for gold leaf, and the crystals of gum Arabic that help control the flow of the colours.

Quite soon I was able to compose individual letters that took up the space of an entire page. Delicate violets, about-to-bloom roses, purple peonies, and other flowers wove themselves around, behind and in front of my letters. Sister was astounded: "You have a wonderful understanding of how the letters were living things for those long-dead artists. Your flowers and vegetation flow naturally from the shapes of the letters and never overwhelm them."

I LOVE LUCY versus *I REMEMBER MAMA*: Monday nights at eight p.m. were Lucy's. Madame Beaulieu and I giggled and laughed through each episode. Every week we waited for Lucy to put herself into yet another outrageous situation in order to wiggle her way out. We were seldom disappointed.

I Remember Mama on Friday evening was very different. At the end of the work week I yearned to travel to San Francisco to the warm comfort of those Norwegian immigrants and the mother who loved and cared for them all. The plaintive music of Grieg always put me in the best mood to understand the plight of the children who relied on their mother — herself homesick for the old ways — to alleviate their bouts of unhappiness.

Marta's lined face betrayed the hard life of an immigrant; her voice was soft and gentle, always alert to comfort her husband and children. She allowed neither her spouse nor offspring even a glance at her own trials and tribulations.

As I looked at the program week after week, I would covertly glance over to Madame Beaulieu and realize that she looked like Peggy Wood as Marta Hansen. Not only did the two women braid their hair and place it at the top of their heads, they were eager listeners to what others told them. Nels, Mama's son, was gauche and naïve, but his mother adored him. He must have reminded me of myself.

IMITATION OF CHRIST versus THE LIVES OF THE SAINTS: Four or five times a week we were read to during meals at the Orphanage in Toronto. In this way, we were reminded of our Catholic heritage; most of us thought it was to exact payment for our repasts — meagre though they were.

Thomas à Kempis was a first-rate masochist as well as a dull writer. How I inwardly groaned when we had to listen to his tedious discourses on the life of Christ. Perhaps it is because of him that I have so much difficulty with all representations of the adult Christ, particularly the Sacred Heart with the named body part placed outside the chest.

Stories about the escapades of the saints were completely different. Most of these people had brazenly embraced a wide assortment of tortures. Narratives about racks and wheels, fingernails being torn out, and various body parts being mutilated were grist for our young mills. We all hankered for these accounts. We did not believe the stories as much as we celebrated the inventiveness of the writers who had created such improbable adventures.

INTROVERT: A friend once told me: "You are a very unusual person, Étienne."

"Most people think me strange."

"Strange — as in odd?"

"Exactly. That is my reputation."

"There is a saying. *To be different is a sign of genius.*"

"That is not how I see it. I have always been an introvert, someone who is said to live comfortably only in his own head."

INVITATIONS: Often difficult to refuse.

Mr. Sanders, the manager of my branch ten years ago, was a pleasure to work for: everyone in the Bank said so: janitors, assistant managers, the tellers. One of my colleagues claimed our boss was a "straight arrow — says what he means, does as he says." Sanders had a good word for everyone. He thanked us for the smallest accomplishments as if we had showered vast, surprising riches upon him.

Tall, angular Sanders must in his youth have been an athlete. Rising quickly at the Royal had taken a toll on him — that was plain to see. His nose was bloodshot, his eyes often half-closed. Although no one ever witnessed him imbibing on the job, everyone was certain he was drinking himself to death. Poor man and poor us, we thought: he won't last long.

Sanders was absent from the Bank more than most managers. "I have more and more useless meetings to attend at head office," he lamented. Once, however, when an emergency arose, he could not be reached at the contact number he had left. The startled clerk at the other end of the line acted as if there were no meetings Mr. Sanders ever need attend.

I got along well with Sanders, who made a point of calling me Étienne. Occasionally he even spoke to me in French, a language he knew well. Despite good relations, I was surprised when he called me into his office one afternoon, motioning me to close the door. He even asked me to sit down, signalling a long conversation. I was certain that I was about to be fired.

The manager hemmed and hawed for a while, speaking first about the dreadful winter we were experiencing. He then began lecturing me on economics, a subject about which I know absolutely nothing. Finally, he looked at me intently, his eyes getting even puffier in the process.

"I have a terrible predicament before me. I have to make a decision that is not in my best interest."

I stared back at him and waited for the sad story of the reasons for my termination to unfold.

Apparently oblivious to my feelings, Sanders continued: "The Bank has asked me to go to Shanghai on a very important mission. This is the most important request ever made of me. A successful mission would open doors previously closed."

I had no idea why he would begin the sad news about me in such a roundabout way.

"I cannot go to China. I have concealed from the Bank that my wife is Chinese, a refugee from Mao's revolution. If I was to travel there and that truth was uncovered, I would be detained — perhaps permanently."

I had met Mrs. Sanders on two occasions — she spoke hardly a word of English. I also knew that she had been born in Hangzhou.

"I have informed the Bank that I have recently been diagnosed with a peptic ulcer and am therefore unable to be of service. When I told my supervisor, he was not pleased, although he understood that the kind of commitment I had made to my job could result in health problems. He shrugged his shoulders and said, 'You'll just have to find someone completely trustworthy to go in your place.'"

I still did not see the purpose in my being told this complicated story.

"Étienne, I have decided that you shall go to Shanghai."

He did not ask or entreat: he commanded.

"In six weeks or so, you will be on your way to China. I shall train you for your assignment there. In essence, you will be verifying the complicated financial transactions involved in selling an enormous amount of wheat to China. You will work in a building on the Bund, maintain regular office hours and be there about six weeks. Nothing could be simpler."

Nothing simpler? I thought.

I gulped loudly. Sanders looked me directly in the eye.

"I'll be happy to be of service," I assured him. Fear consumed me. How would I ever survive in that sin-filled city?

Madame Beaulieu would veto my proposed trip. Of that I was sure. Once she did, I would find grounds on which to renege.

IRONY: A concept — saying the opposite of what you really mean — that often evades my understanding. Ditto for sarcasm. I have never understood why people cannot simply say what they mean and have done with it.

ISOLATION: The most vital question in the life of any artist. Does he abandon the world in order to use his time to create? If he does so, does he have anything to write about? A chicken and egg issue, I suppose.

In my case, I am not sure I have any choice. I must work a full week to sustain myself. I have almost no spare money. I find it difficult to make friends. I'm not sure I can claim to enjoy my own company best. Sometimes I think my existence as a loner has been willy-nilly thrust upon me. Other times I see myself as merely perverse.

These days my thoughts are with that strange man Vincent van Gogh. He was so lucky to have a brother, Theo, to whom he could confide his innermost thoughts.

So you must not think that I disavow things: I am rather faithful in my unfaithfulness, and though changed, I am the same, and my only anxiety is: how can I be of use in the world, cannot I serve some purpose and be of any good, how can I learn more and study certain subjects profoundly?

Our inward thoughts, do they ever show outwardly? There may be great fire in our soul, but no one ever comes to warm himself at it, and the passersby see only a little smoke coming through the chimney, and pass on their way. One must tend that inward fire, have salt in oneself, wait patiently yet with how much impatience for the hour when somebody will come and sit down near it ...

Would that I had such an inward fire! How much comfort it must have given him! What I share with that great artist is a tendency to be, as he put it, *"very backward and narrow-minded."*

If I had even a small portion of the Dutch painter's sense of purpose, I could find a measure of the salvation that eludes me. Interest I have; commitment, I fear, I do not possess in sufficient quantity.

Kirk Douglas in *Lust for Life* is naïve and generous — a combination that means one will have a tragic destiny in the real world. Anthony Quinn as Gauguin is canny and selfish — the combination that always guarantees success. No wonder poor Vincent cut his ear off. James Donald did a good job playing the perplexed, ever-generous Theo. As I sat in the movie theatre watching the triumphs and tragedies of Van Gogh's life unfold, I was awestruck by the peculiar beauty of his art. That afternoon in the movie theatre I implored heaven to grant me such dedication. Oh, to be able to give one's life in such a noble cause! Such pure selfishness, such pure selflessness!

ITINERARY: To my considerable astonishment, Madame Beaulieu was overjoyed that I had been given such an important assignment by the Bank. "It is about time your talents were recognized. The bushel has been hidden for far too long!" (Politely, I did not point out that she did not understand the Biblical metaphor.) When I objected to her enthusiastic endorsement of the trip, she shoo-shooed me. "Your opportunity has at last presented itself. You must seize it!" Perhaps unfairly, I suspected that Madame Beaulieu's enthusiasm for my sojourn in China was assisted by the fact that Isabelle and her mother were about to descend on her for a visit. If I were away, my room could be used by Isabelle and perhaps mitigate some family quarrels.

Sanders quickly prepared me for my duties in Shanghai. In co-operation with the Royal Bank and the Wheat Board, the federal government was selling an unprecedented amount of Canada's largest crop to China. "Every farm and co-operative that is part of the deal must be accounted for," he told me. "We must be vigilant to ensure that no frauds of any kind take place. In addition, you must record where the wheat is sent. We suspect a large portion of it is being sent to Eastern Europe. None of our business if the peasants in China are left to starve while their Communist brothers in Albania are given their food. We must simply record the 'from' and 'to' piles — a bit like sorting mail, if you catch my drift." I did understand.

Wouldn't some of the documents be in Chinese? I asked. Obviously, I hoped this would prove a deterrent to my carrying out the assignment. "Nothing to worry about. Numbers are numbers. Someone will be assigned to translate whatever details you have to know. Nothing simpler." Very easy for him to say. He was not exchanging the security of home for life behind an Iron Curtain.

J

J is in a constantly confused emotional state since I has stolen so much from it. Do I really belong in the alphabet? it must ask itself on a daily basis. J gets its revenge because its upward hook allows it a bit of a swagger, a boastful edge to its personality.

JARVIS STREET: The lower end near the market is full of bustle; to the north are demure middle-class houses and further up, past Carlton, are the stately mansions of the Cawthras, the Masseys and the Gooderhams. The other day I came across a clipping I saved from *The Globe and Mail* just after I arrived here: "During the past two decades, Jarvis Street has been deserted by many of its old and respected residents and its thirteen licensed hotels, eight of them in one block, have spread its shady reputation as the heart of the city's tenderloin district ... Policemen patrol their beats in pairs ... Bootleggers, prostitutes and dope peddlers have made their headquarters in its big old rooming houses and apartments." True enough, but villainy gives a city character.

If I wish to remind myself of the human propensity to revel in civic bad taste, I take a walk on Jarvis or on nearby Yonge, where I can observe seediness in its full glory. I obviously have a depraved side, but I enjoy the sumptuous purples and deep yellows I glimpse on these streets, where most people seem to be indulging themselves.

JUMPY: My flight to London by way of BOAC was on a Saturday evening in November 1957. After that twelve-hour crossing, I would have to wait four hours on Sunday afternoon at Heathrow for the Aeroflot plane that would take me to Moscow. There, I would have a wait of six hours until leaving for Shanghai (this plane would put down once in Inner Mongolia for refuelling). I would arrive in China forty-eight hours after leaving Toronto.

When I showed up for work on the Friday before my flight, Sanders called me into his office. "Take the day off, Étienne. You must have many arrangements still to make."

I assured him I was completely prepared. "Still, you need to relax before the ordeal of three long flights. Go home and put your feet up. The Bank is very, very appreciative of your efforts." From the top drawer of his desk he retrieved two one-hundred-dollar bills. "Just our way of saying thanks." He wished me good luck on my assignment and shook my hand vigorously. As I was about to leave his office, he scratched his head. "I almost forgot

— the wife would have given me hell." He then handed me a bulky parcel. "This vase is a gift to her brother. Could you deliver it for her?" I agreed to this. Sanders cautioned me. "You know what the Commies are like. Very nosy. Try to keep this out of sight in case your luggage is inspected. Perhaps you could squirrel it away."

On Saturday I was filled with a sense of dread. Madame Beaulieu insisted on supervising my packing to ensure I was taking along all the necessary clothing. Perhaps I felt guilty about buying the camera, but my nerves were fraught. "You have never been on an airplane before, and you are going to a strange place," she informed me. "Everything will be okay. You will transport yourself well." The Beaulieus insisted on driving me to Toronto Airport, although I wondered if their battered, six-year-old Cadillac would carry us there safely. My farewell to the family was filled with tears — most of them shed by Madame Beaulieu.

Once I was welcomed aboard the plane by a stewardess greeting me in a plummy British accent, I thought I might relax. The seat next to me was unoccupied, and I did not have to engage in trivial conversation. I spent my time anticipating the fate that awaited me in Shanghai. I envisioned a city of great darkness: narrow, crowded streets; police and military men everywhere; spies watching my every move. I shuddered. Unlike the city Tintin visited, there might be fewer rickshaws, opium dens, and other remnants of Shanghai's fabled decadence. There certainly would be no Snowy to bestow unconditional canine love upon me.

K is very much a lone wolf in the alphabet world. To be honest, it is an outcast because its functionality, especially at the beginning of words, has been unceremoniously stolen by C. Nevertheless, K has reaped some glory because designers often fall in love with its lower diagonal and embellish it with considerable flourish. Even the lowly of this world can always find a measure of recompense.

Yet troubles persist for this member of the alphabet. Kafka, intimately acquainted with the letter, once wrote: "I find the letter K offensive, almost nauseating." Was he really writing about himself?

KALEIDOSCOPES: I love the ways in which such simple toys reassemble the world in their playful ways. The tube, filled with mirrors and beads or pebbles, allows us to reinvent our ordinary worlds.

KASPAR HAUSER: Dishevelled and smelly, a young man appeared on the streets of Nuremberg, Germany, in May 1828. He smiled, walked hesitantly, and would eat only bread flushed down with water. A note attached to his clothing gave his name but little more. The only words to escape his lips were, "I do not know." Later he recalled living in a dark cell with only a straw bed and wooden toy horse. He had been drugged when his clothes were changed or his hair cut. He did not know how he had arrived at the town.

Subsequently, Kaspar became an object of curiosity. Arguments raged as to his identity, various people wanted to be his patron; he was taken into the care of a kindly schoolteacher. In 1829, an unknown person attempted to kill him with an axe, badly wounding his forehead. Four years later he was stabbed fatally in the chest. The headstone at his gravesite reads, "Here lies Kaspar Hauser, riddle of his time. His birth was unknown, his death mysterious."

I am a riddle to myself. I have never been subjected to the inhumane regime inflicted upon Hauser. But, like him, I do not know how I became the person I am. What is the mystery ailment in my soul that keeps me so desperately apart from others?

KENNEDY: Even in Canada we were badly shaken by his death, by its brutality. At home, all of us remained glued to the television set; all of us burst into tears when, at the funeral, the president's tiny son waved his father farewell. The Americans lost their Camelot, but in Toronto we felt that our lives had been badly tarnished.

KERNEL: "Unless a grain of seed die, it cannot bear fruit." This apparent paradox is my favourite saying from the New Testament. The kernel must be watered, broken down and destroyed; unless the cycle of death is undergone, no birth can take place.

I sometimes wonder if this observation by Christ contains the key to the mystery of life. If something in us is not destroyed, we spend our life in vain. The only prayer I ever utter is a request for this blessing to be given to me.

KIM: Kipling's hero is a literary orphan of whom I approve, although he is a bit of a schemer. Nevertheless, he is resourceful, inventive, and adaptable — qualities I wish I possessed. An exceptionally clever little chap, he attaches himself to a series of father figures. The impish monkey boy is the consummate survivor.

KITTEN: At the orphanages, we obviously did not have pets. Luc was allergic to dogs and cats and so there was no family animal. I cannot say I ever desperately wanted a puppy or a kitten, but I would not have minded.

I had been living with the Beaulieus for about three months when, one late June afternoon, when I was walking home from work, I noticed a scrawny yellow tabby kitten following me. More a young teenager than a real youngster, he carried himself with the street-smart elegance of an animal that has had to fend for itself. I turned around, knelt down, and waited for him to come to me, which he did at once. Before allowing me to touch him, he brushed himself against my knee. He was inspecting me as a possible owner and obviously liked what he saw: he purred his applause loudly. I looked around to see if I could see any sign of an owner. The kitten, I decided, was a stray.

I rose to my feet and continued on my way. The kitten continued his pursuit, although twice I turned around to shoo him away. He would have none of that.

Smugly aware of the devotion I had inspired, I continued walking, basking in the knowledge that this little creature was taken with me. I knew that I could not befriend him, but I paid no attention to this glaring fact of life.

I came to a busy corner and waited for the traffic to clear. Driven by his assuredness of the goodness of the world in having given him someone to care for him, the kitten ran ahead into traffic. He was hit by a car, thrown into the air and landed on the ground. Once or twice he leapt up, blood streaming from his mouth. I remember that his copper-coloured eyes met mine. "You have betrayed me," they shouted. When I got to his side, he was dead. I moved his still warm corpse out of the street and onto a patch of green near the sidewalk.

Distraught, I burst into tears. Here was a creature who had loved me. I had been complacent about his future, like some wanton lover dallying with a casual pickup. And now he was dead, his little corpse just starting to stiffen. I had been a neglectful parent to this scrappy little outcast.

L

L is, like its shape, narrow in outlook.

LAUREL AND HARDY: Madame Beaulieu thinks these two are gifted comics. I despise them. The fat one — a brash American — is always tormenting the thin one, who speaks in a quasi-English accent.

I keep my mouth firmly shut when this couple appears on our small screen at home and excuse myself as soon as I can. If, as I have read, comedy is built upon sorrow and discord, these men are geniuses.

LEFTOVERS: Not as in food from one meal that is preserved so that it can be eaten later. At the Orphanage, anyone who stayed beyond their seventh year was a "leftover." Such boys and girls were not **CUTE**. They were either physically unattractive, had behavioural problems or had refused to co-operate in being placed. We were remnants.

From the time she was five, curly haired, Shirley Temple-looking Carol had been sexually precocious. As a young child, she flirted with men in a suggestive ways; their wives decided they wanted nothing to do with her. Fred the Bully was swarthy: his racial origins were obviously mixed; no one wanted to take a chance with such an obvious question mark. If you did not fit into the adult mindset of what a child was supposed to be — acquiescent, grateful, sweet-tempered — you bore the mark of Cain. How does such a person possibly become an Abel?

LITTLE ORPHAN ANNIE: At the Bank, I am frequently asked if I have seen that day's strip in the *Telegraph*. "A real fighter, that one," somebody once observed. The clear implication was that I should emulate her. A more sensitive person once told me, "That's a real Cinderella story. Rags to riches." That remark is accurate since the heroine is rescued from the claws of Miss Asthma and taken home by Mrs. Warbucks, where-upon that bald-headed giant, Mr. Warbucks, the richest man in the world, returns home from a business trip and is enchanted:

"Say, whose kid are you?"

"I'm nobody's kid. I'm just an orphan Mrs. Warbucks took home on trial."

"WHAT? On trial, eh? Don't you ever dare to call me Mr. Warbucks again. You call me DADDY, see?"

Mr. Warbucks, it turns out, is the feckless sort. Sometimes he disappears from Annie's life for months at a time, although he often appears as a *deus ex machina*. Since Harold Gray, Annie's creator, began the strip in 1924, he has had to invent all kinds of adventures to keep his readers coming back for more.

I have always been suspicious of Mr. Warbucks, who looks like a bully. Annie can usually rely on her dog, Sandy, but once that animal went missing. The dog was gone for so long that the cartoonist was flooded with sackfuls of letters. One communication was a telegram from Dearborn, Michigan: "Please do all you can to help Annie find Sandy." It was signed "Henry Ford."

My reservations about Annie are considerable. I particularly dislike the garish red colour of her hair and the empty circles that make up her eyes. Yet, I do admire the way she creatively extricates herself from difficult situations. She never feels sorry for herself. For that reason, I much prefer her to Charlotte Brontë's self-righteous Jane Eyre.

LEOPARDS: Famous for never being able to change their spots. These mammals are often cited in any debate over nature versus nurture. They are made a certain way and can never remove, bleach or whiten those black spots. In reading a recent issue of *National Geographic*, I gather that they are very elusive prey on safari. They camouflage themselves well and, of course, they are assisted in this endeavour by those very same markings. One adventurer, an amateur wildlife enthusiast, took dozens of photos of several of these beasts, proudly submitted them to the *New York Times* and was thoroughly humiliated when the Nature editor informed him he had photographed cheetahs.

LION: The King of Beasts. Many issues of *National Geographic* have wonderful colour photos of these noble animals. A few months back I was moved to tears by one showing a father standing guard over his little progeny. His mane proudly waving in the breeze, the parent stared at his beautiful little cub. How I have always wanted to have been so treasured by a proud father.

A few days later, I was heartbroken when I read the text accompanying the illustration. The male lion had just murdered the infant cub. If you looked closely, you could see the strangulation marks around the cub's neck. The lion had recently defeated the father of the cub in his amorous pursuit of the baby's mother. Having achieved that end, he wanted to have his own cub and in order to do so he had to destroy the other lion's progeny so that his new mate would come into heat.

Oh! The infinite horror between appearance and reality!

LUCK: Sometimes I have some. Not very often but often enough that it takes my breath away. In fact, meeting Chang borders more on the miraculous than the lucky.

The BOAC flight was tedious; the wait in London for the Aeroflot plane that would take me to Moscow passed quickly enough; I entered a narrow prison when I was shown to my seat by the unsmiling, unfriendly attendant. I expected that I would be fed only bread and water en route to the USSR I was not completely wrong in making that assumption. The greyness of Moscow airport was a continuation of that experience: this was *the* Cold War I was always reading about.

The interior of the plane taking me to China was deep red.

My spirit soared, although I must admit that I slept for most of the final leg of my journey. When I awoke, the plane was preparing to land in a country that was synonymous in my mind with blue and grey.

If I had expected dark, gloomy skies in Shanghai, I was rudely disappointed. Clear, bright sunshine overwhelmed me as I awoke from my long snooze. I wandered off the plane, had my passport and other papers examined at least four times by various levels of officialdom, and then headed for the exit. My attention was distracted by all kinds of military personnel — women as well as men — carrying submachine guns. My worst fears, I was certain, were about to be fulfilled. Then I noticed the fellow holding the sign labelled "ÉTIENNE."

I knew that someone would meet me at Shanghai Airport. I had not suspected that the person in question would be my age — or that his entire face would be consumed by a wide-open, eager smile. His jet-black hair, piercing brown, slanted eyes and squat nose were the exact opposite of my own features, although he was my exact height and also of slight build.

"Étienne, I have been much anticipating your arrival." Chang said this as he clasped me in a vice-like embrace. "You are most welcome here. I shall do everything in my power to service you." He then motioned me in the direction of our car and driver. To my surprise, the Royal Bank Cadillac was a perfectly conditioned model of the scruffy automobile the Beaulieus had used to drive to Toronto Airport.

We loaded my luggage and settled into the backseat. Chang issued some orders to the driver, and we were on our way in the direction of the Bund, where the Royal office was located.

I cannot say I noticed much of anything on the drive, but completely absent was the sense of desperation I had expected to glimpse on the face of everyone I encountered in Shanghai. People were everywhere — bicycles abounded, men and women were actually dressed in drab blues and greys — but everyone had a purpose. That was a phenomenon seldom witnessed in Toronto.

LUNA: As in lunatic. A few years ago I looked through some old issues of the Montreal *Gazette* at the Toronto Public Library and confirmed what I had long suspected: I was born under a full moon. Should I be happy or sad? Am I a madman pure and simple?

LURE: A very good name for the tackle designed to lead fish to their deaths. When the word is used as a verb, I think of moths being attracted to the flames. I think of myself as someone seduced by the magic world of drawing.

LURID: As in both horrid and gaudy. One of the most fascinating accounts I have heard of fakery concerns one of Mao's chief ministers. This man, fascinated by Western artists of the calibre of Van Gogh and Munch, routinely has paintings stolen on his behalf by henchmen in Europe and the United States. Once the painting is removed from a museum — usually in a daring daytime heist — it is smuggled into China through a cargo ship docking in Shanghai.

Then, the necessity of secrecy really asserts itself because the Chairman would be deeply offended if he learned that one of his chief subordinates was a collector of decadent Capitalist art, pictures that contain not the slightest hint of social realism.

All the canvases are kept in an underground chamber guarded by loyal and high-paid subordinates. Chang told me that the paintings are all brightly coloured, the walls of the gallery a deep, exceptionally gaudy magenta.

What the great collector is supremely unaware of is that years ago Interpol, having tracked the thefts to his doorstep and, as a result, having undertaken a careful study of his taste for the garish, had had all canvases to which he would be drawn removed from the walls of the various museums and substituted excellent replicas. The secret collection is almost entirely made up of fakes.

LUXURY: During the one hour drive from the airport, Chang told me our office was in the North China Daily News Building, "smack dab" in the middle of the Bund. I would be living with him on Henan Zhong Lu, only three blocks away from the office. "You will be very comfortably accommodated, as you will soon discover."

My new acquaintance informed me that he would act as my translator. "In fact, I shall be your factotum — I shall be everything you need to accomplish your tasks." Only then did I have the presence of mind to ask his name: "My full name is Chang Chon-Ren. You may call me Chang. Nothing could be simpler — or easier to remember."

He later told me he had been born in a small town in Jiangsu province; his mother died when he was two, his father when he was three. He retained no memory of them. He was brought up by his mother's parents. The three of them moved to Nanjing, the former capital, in 1936, when he was four. During the Japanese massacre of Nanjing in December 1937, the three of them had escaped to Shanghai where he was fortunate enough to finish school. Later, for one year, he had attended classes in English and Accounting at Fudan University. Ever since then, he had "improvised" his existence, "doing this and doing that."

China, he impressed upon me, was a country based upon *jiade*, fakery. People had false identities, identity cards, passports; cheating and gulling were common occurrences. "I can tell you one thing about myself, I do not deal in *jiade* of any kind."

Behind the Bund, the streets changed character: they were narrow and congested. The shabby lane houses at which the Cadillac pulled up frightened me. The exteriors of all the dwellings were filthy and in various stages of advanced decay; at each entrance but ours men sat around smoking and glancing idly in our direction. One met my stare, turned away and spat. Some of the children playing in the street were intrigued for a few moments by my pale face and then continued what they were doing.

If Chang noticed my dismay, he offered no comment. We removed my luggage from the trunk of the car, and he quickly bid the driver goodbye. He then took out his key to open the door. Fearing the worst, I closed my eyes, bracing myself for the horrors I was about to confront.

Breathing — and perhaps sighing — deeply, I was dumbfounded to behold a series of interconnecting rooms sparingly but carefully furnished. The two sofas in the first room were upholstered in what was obviously expensive material; the chairs and tables were from the Ming dynasty and looked like pieces of furniture I had seen in books. All of these rooms had large windows at the back that faced south on to a walled garden filled with spectacular plants and small ponds.

Witnessing — and obviously chuckling to himself at — my amazement, Chang observed that our landlady loved contrast. "She likes to surprise visitors with what she calls her 'folly' — keeping this perfect little house in the midst of 'Red destruction.'"

M

M can be thought of as a **V** with supporting legs. Not a nice prospect for a letter to contemplate, as if its existence is derived from another's. Its many strokes make it a designer's nightmare. However, its shape is derived from the Egyptian owl, bestowing upon it a special brand of wisdom. For that reason, I love words filled with **M**; its heavy liquid sound promises common sense and truth.

In almost every language, **M** reminds the reader of the person to whom he was born: *mat* (Russian), *matr* (Sanskrit), *moeder* (Dutch), *mater* (Latin), and so on. I once read the root origin is from the Indo-European *mamma*, which refers to the mother's breast. We remain so hungry for the nourishment that can be provided only by suckling that we make the word for that person unswervingly similar.

Yet, as I have learned all too well, **M** is associated with danger and intrigue. Is there any more attention-grabbing title in the history of cinema than *Dial M for Murder*?

MACHIAVELLIAN: Few people in history have been so tarred and feathered as Niccolò di Bernardo dei Machiavelli, who wrote the wrong book at the wrong time. He simply wanted to point out that cunning was sometimes a necessary ingredient in the repertoire of a successful politician. Rather than being praised for authoring a book of helpful hints, he has been vilified as the proponent of expediency over morality.

In my opinion, politicians, businessmen and lawyers would have uncovered the lore of unscrupulous manipulation and extreme mendacity without the assistance of a how-to manual. Machiavelli's case is a clear example of killing the messenger.

I have no access to any real secrets at the Bank, but, even if I were privy to such information, lacking any capacity for guile, I could not make use of it. I do not make this statement in a self-righteous way in praise of my own virtue. I think some capacity for dissembling (not necessarily lying) is probably essential to success in any vocation.

MACHINATIONS: I soon learned that Chang was in essence the Royal Bank of Canada in China. A certain Boris Harper — whom I never saw — was the nominal head, but he hardly ever appeared in the single large room that was the Royal head-quarters in Shanghai. He had purchased some sort of sinecure from the Bank, collected a large amount for his services and then hired Chang, at a measly salary, to run the operation.

Harper, through his family connections to the great Jewish families of Shanghai, was supposed to have the necessary wherewithal to manage the Reds if they attempted to interfere.

My work was simple enough — though demanding. Thousands of individual bills of sale from Canadian farmers were inspected by me and then assigned to one of the buyers (most of them were from Albania); Chang and I would then invoice the buyers. When payment was made, the various consignments of wheat — on their way to Shanghai — would be released; payment of the individual invoices would then be made by the Bank to the Wheat Board and then paid to the sellers. A cumbersome, time-consuming, inefficient process.

MADNESS: Racism is its ugliest incarnation. Aryans slaughtering Jews: that is the incomprehensible crime of the twentieth century, but Chang told me in horrifying, graphic detail about the Japanese slaughter of 300,000 Chinese at Nanjing in 1937, a crime worthy, he maintained, of Hitler. He finds it difficult to forgive, especially as the Japanese government has never offered a genuine apology.

In comparison, I suppose, the humiliation the French-Canadian has suffered at the hands of English Canada might seem — to some — mild.

MARILYN MONROE: I was deeply saddened when she died five years ago. Her baby voice always had such a tender sadness in it, even in *Gentlemen Prefer Blondes* and *Some Like It Hot*. She was what is known as a "bombshell" or an "It girl" because men found her so alluring, but many women were saddened by her passing. The only person I know who actively disliked her was Tante Isabelle, who said she was beneath contempt. "That woman is such a tramp — I did not like the way she led on the married man in *The Seven Year Itch*." For Tante Isabelle, all of Hollywood's sirens — especially Ava Gardner and Rita Hayworth — were contemptible, "no better than call girls." Even mild-mannered Frank Beaulieu smiled warily at his sister-in-law's inability to distinguish between life and art.

MARTA: Like everyone else, I went to the movie of *The Sound of Music* to be entranced by Julie Andrews as the rejected, would-be novice who eventually falls in love with Christopher Plummer and escapes with him and his brood from the clutches of the Nazis. I longed to be wafted into that world and to hear all the musical set pieces in their correct order (I knew them all from the radio).

What I was not prepared for was Peggy Wood as the stern but warm-hearted Mother Superior. I could still catch a glimpse of Marta Hansen, but the actress had shrunken in size, and I had the unhappy thought that she might not be long for this world.

MASKS: We wear them all the time — not just at Halloween. Necessary camouflage in our daily battles. Who wishes to be seen as they really are when the potential for being shamed or humiliated is infinite?

MATISSE: Flat grounds, vivid colours, abstract shapes. Those are the critical terms applied to him by art historians, as if a series of meaningless phrases could encapsulate a great artist. The truth is that all genuine artists — although they have vastly different personalities — always remain in touch with the adolescent within them.

ME: Chang and I were walking along the Henshan Road, a place that became famous in "degenerate" films made before 1949. Behind high walls, the lights in the mansions glittered, casting a spell on us. Chang explained that a new set of residents — CP faithful — had taken over these buildings. "The new rascals have chased out the old rascals. Nothing ever changes in China."

Sometimes Chang grilled me. "Have you ever been intimate with a woman?" he asked, changing subjects abruptly.

"No. I have never been — as you put it — intimate with anyone."

"Why is that, I suppose?"

Now I felt like I was being interrogated by Inspector Charlie Chan of the Honolulu Police Department, the erstwhile Confucian philosopher. "I have sexual feelings, of course. I have once or twice been infatuated with some of the women I work with. They showed no interest in me. I am bashful. Nothing happened."

"Is the matter as simple as that?"

"For one thing, I was not that interested in them. I am essentially a loner."

I do not know if Chang was dissatisfied with my answers — this was the longest conversation we had ever had.

MEEK: Blessed they may be, but they will never inherit the earth.

METAMORPHOSIS: What a glorious word! The stories in Ovid, even the most far-fetched ones, never cease to enthrall me. In nature an ugly wormlike creature becomes a Monarch.

Of course, anyone who sets out to be an artist is, by definition, hoping for an Ovidian miracle by which the dross that is his work will be elevated into the realm of art. Many set out on this rigorous path — unfortunately, few are chosen. I fear I am one of the unlucky. What a dire fate: ultimately an admirer of art but no artist.

MIRACLE: Not as in ladies sawed in half by magicians, no matter they are as talented as Mr. Blackstone. The raising of Lazarus from the dead? Perhaps, but I am skeptical this event ever took place. Bread and wine transformed into the body and blood of Christ? I have serious reservations, *pace* Madame Beaulieu.

I have no doubt whatsoever that Henri Rousseau's childish-looking application of paints to canvas led to the creation of a number of miracles.

MOSAICS: If I could travel to Byzantium, I would learn the craft of placing brightly coloured jewel-like pieces of stone — the ungrouted *tesserae* or *smalti* — next to each other. A few days ago I perused a book that reproduced the famous Christ Pancreator from Hagia Sophia. There he is looking both sternly and apprehensively at the onlooker. If anyone could restore my lost faith, it would be that man. On the next few pages were close-ups of parts of Jesus's face, but those photographs looked like abstract paintings.

Imitation being the sincerest form of flattery, I began yesterday an experiment. I drew three portraits composed of coloured squares. If I scrutinized the results on my desk, they looked like simple, bright, pleasing arrangements of colours but when I pinned them to the wall and walked back a few feet, they were transformed into faces.

N

N requires a quiet, domestic understanding among its three parts. Otherwise, it would collapse. This letter is also aware of its crucial position as the fourteenth letter of twenty-six, realizing full well it must demonstrate responsibility and maturity as the representative of the alphabet's middle age.

NAME: A year ago I came upon Marc Tremblay, one of the orphans from long ago in Montreal. Now a professor at Queen's in Kingston, he was adopted by a couple who lived in Whitby. We chatted for about half an hour. I do not recall much of what we said, but I was startled when he mentioned in passing that his Christian name was now M-A-R-K. "Why is that?" I asked. "My adoptive parents told me that I could retain my surname but that they didn't want me going through life spelling my first name incorrectly."

NATURE: It takes away a bit from us year by year. Art remains untouched.

NOVELTY: The Hasselblad was such a new part of my existence that the prospect of actually using it appalled me. At first, I refused to carry it with me when exploring Shanghai with Chang.

"That is a very unusual camera you have. Is it special or expensive?"

"Both. It is a precision-made instrument made almost by hand in Sweden. You flip the top cover open and then look down onto the ground glass to see the image you are photographing."

He especially liked the grey-blue leather in which the camera was housed. "Have you recently purchased it?"

I admitted that I had obtained it shortly before coming away. "Then why are you not using it?"

"I would feel self-conscious wearing it."

"But self-consciousness is a good thing, no?"

As usual, I found it difficult to argue with Chang when he — in his best Chinese manner — reversed all my phobias. Everything I considered bad, he saw as good. Under his silent pressure, I began to take the camera along when we visited such sites as the Yu Gardens, Hongkou Park, and the Jade Buddha Temple.

As my third weekend in Shanghai approached, I boldly informed Chang that I would like to wander around the city by myself. He said nothing, but I knew he was pleased that the caged bird sought his freedom.

That weekend I travelled to the Hongkou district — the Japanese Concession — to look at the dreary places where many of the Jewish émigrés from Hitler's Germany had been inconveniently settled by the Japanese; later, I wandered through the International Settlement and the French Concession. The Chinese simply ignored me. The men, as usual, spat in the street, the women berated the men, and the children scrambled as soon as an adult took notice of them. No one cared a whit for me or the strange camera hung around my neck; they paid no attention when I stopped in my tracks, looked down to the ground glass to take their pictures and then wandered away.

Before I arrived in Shanghai I had known it was not — by Chinese standards — an old city. I had been told the best buildings were Western. Although aware of that, I still became fascinated by the startling contrast between the architecture and the people. I had never been to Paris, but many of the buildings looked Parisian. Perhaps if I had been to France I would not have had the vulgar thought that I was in a Europe that had been taken over by the Chinese.

NOVENA: As a child, I had been taught the efficacy of this special kind of series of prayers, which are said nine days in a row. Basically, we would recite the rosary to some entity such as Our Lady of Perpetual Sorrow. Our objectives were lofty, usually World Peace. In order to give the novenas the solemnity they deserved, they were performed in church, almost always followed by a liberal dashing of hymns accompanied by incense.

This particular childhood memory might have been extinguished if I had not met Rose at the Toronto Public Library.

Like me, she frequented the art history section. Considerably older than me, I would guess she was at least seventy the first time I set eyes on her. A small, wizened woman with an enormous beak of a nose, her messy hair was pure white; she also walked with a noticeable stoop due to dowager's hump. At first, Hansel-like, I was wary of her because she reminded me of the witch in the Grimm Brothers' fairy tale. She sometimes annoyed me because she would remove from the shelves a book or two that I wanted to peruse. She would simply gaze at one image or another for hours on end. Although she had a large notebook with her, I never saw her open it to enter a reflection.

I may have been irritated as well because Rose was one of the numerous people who used the library as a daytime refuge from the streets. In winter, these people occupied almost every sitting space available, from which strong, dank smells emanated.

I must have beheld Rose for a year or two before I ever spoke to her. One Saturday afternoon, she hobbled over to where I was sitting and asked if I would soon be finished with a book on Holbein. Seeing the urgency in her expression, I surrendered the book to her. Two weeks later, I encountered her when I was arriving at the library. She gave me an eager, welcoming smile and then vanished inside. A month later, she wandered over to where I was seated. She remarked that she had noticed I liked Van Gogh. When I nodded in agreement, she informed me I had excellent taste.

Our relationship now consisted in the exchange of pleasantries until — perhaps four months later — she asked if we might meet outside the library for lunch at the greasy spoon across the street. I assumed correctly that she hoped I would pay, which of course I did.

Rose was not given to idle pleasantries. She told me that she had worked as a secretary at Dominion Paper until she was sixty, at which time she was let go. Having been a person of "high rectitude and considerable order," as she put it, she broke down when she no longer had employment.

Nowadays, she informed me, there were only two constants in her life: the Church (she attended Mass and received Communion daily) and art. As proof of the latter, she asked if I would like to see some of her sketches. I could hardly refuse. As I leafed through the pages, I could see that she had drawn — using only Crayolas — variants on a series of masterpieces she had surveyed intently in art books.

Unlike Cedric Smith, she made no attempt to replicate the pictures she had seen with any exactitude. Rather, she had rendered artists like Giotto and Brueghel in the ways a child might reinvent them. Her pictures were, she insisted, "adaptations — my way of looking at pictures." They were certainly crude: the colours were often harsh, the lines not completely thought out. Yet in each, she had caught the essence of what she was imitating and, in the process, infused her own spirit.

I told Rose I was captivated. In fact — I do not know what came over me — I confessed to her that I too spent a great deal of my time drawing. That came as no surprise to her, she insisted. "One artist always knows another." In fact, as we got ready to return to the library, she told me that she intended to begin a Novena on my behalf. "I am going to ask Our Lady to inspire you."

The following week I took some of my drawings to show her. She was not there. When she had not reappeared for a month, I summoned up my courage to ask one of the librarians if she had noticed that Rose had been absent for a long time. "Miss Perkins? The poor dear was run over by a streetcar."

NOVICE: In Roman Catholic religious orders, an apprentice priest or nun. In a different sense, I always feel like I have only dipped my feet in the water of life. I often ask myself: when am I going to allow the waves — both gentle and fierce — to bounce me back and forth? Like Maria in *The Sound of Music*, I am an extremely bad novice.

NOW: Seems such an easy concept. Life lived in the present moment. The problem is that there is never really any such thing. As soon as the present arrives, it drifts into the past.

There is the common adage: "No good living in the past or building bridges in the future. Live in the present." Do the people who say this realize that they are imposing an impossible task on their listeners?

NUCLEAR FAMILY: Paul Beaulieu was born in 1953, two years after I had moved in with the family. Jean-Pierre — almost three years old — was a bit jealous. Luc, who was in Grade One, was transfixed with the baby. He wanted to take him to school to show to his classmates. If she was exhausted by her new baby, Madame Beaulieu never showed it. "Like you, he has ginger hair," the proud mother pointed out to me time and again.

For the first four months of his life, the infant was colicky. Even I, in my secluded bedroom on the top floor, was woken in the night by the baby's screams. For some reason I have never understood, we all became better natured during this ordeal.

Frank claimed that the *enfant* was taking his time settling in; Madame Beaulieu spent hours each evening walking him. Luc offered to babysit. Jean-Pierre, who eventually insisted on holding the baby on his lap, soon discovered that the difficult baby would stop crying when he held him. To my surprise, the baby was quite taken with me. As soon as he could see, he would smile and reach out to touch my hair, which he would grasp firmly in his hand and then pull.

When Jean-Pierre and I realized that we were Paul's favourites, I volunteered our services. I may have been the official minder, but Jean-Pierre and I spent many contented evenings tending the baby while mother and father took their eldest son to the nearby park.

Madame Beaulieu tells me that she has never been happier than when pregnant or caring for her boys when they were infants. Her joy was boundless when the boys were tiny because she witnessed on a daily basis their pleasure in discovering the wonders of life. "When they became teenagers, they became easily bored," she reflected sadly.

NUDGE: Sometimes a push in the right direction is the only path leading to salvation.

One evening, neither Chang nor I, over-exhausted by our work at the Bank, could sleep, and so we walked in the direction of the Nanjing Road, the centre of the city's thriving night life.

We talked for hours. Rather — Chang talked for hours. My usual inability to converse was glaringly obvious to me. I thought of lots of responses to my friend's observations, but could not find any words to utter. They would not surface — despite my best efforts. Since early childhood, this had been the source of great pain to me — and the reason everyone I knew considered me some sort of idiot.

A series of insults from my past flashed before me.

1. "Why don't you say something? I've just asked you a question."
2. "You can count money rapidly, Étienne, but you have no use for words."
3. "Are you always tongue-tied?"
4. "Your tongue must weigh a ton: it doesn't allow you to make many words."

Sometimes I overcome my inability to utter only robot-like responses, but that is rare. The Beaulieus never commented on this trait of mine — neither did Mrs. Donnelly. With them, I would forget whatever impediment blocked me.

Chang paid no attention whatsoever to my seeming lack of interest in responding. Still, it did not do me any good. I had many things I wanted to say, but my tongue remained resolutely locked.

NUGATORY: An incredibly ugly word perfectly suited to its meanings: futile, trifling, worthless. These are feelings I constantly try to avoid experiencing, and I have begun to wonder if my drawings are a buttress I have constructed to keep them at bay. When I first began the drawings, I sometimes made three or four within the space of a few hours. Nowadays the process takes much longer. I am becoming more of a perfectionist, which is not necessarily a good thing. As I write about China, the same habit of mind infiltrates this memoir. My eye took in so much there that it has prodded my pen to write at greater length.

The old Étienne is disappearing — or is he disintegrating?

NUISANCE: This is just about the harshest word in Madame Beaulieu's vocabulary. Sometimes Frank attracts his wife's use of the word. Tante Isabelle, however, as far as her sister is concerned, has cornered the market in being a pest. "I love my sister," she often begins, "but she is a nuisance."

NUMBNESS: The state to which life often reduces us. We want to feel, but we have been so worn down by unmet expectations, false turns and betrayals that our capacity to feel deeply is destroyed. This is a particularly dangerous terrain for the artist to get stuck in because his work will be of little consequence.

NUMBERS: As a child, I loved them. They gave me a sense of security. Then the security packed up and moved away when I became an adolescent. I can still tell someone instantly what 7898 x 3456 is, but life is not a series of party tricks.

NURSE: Someone who tends to another, not necessarily in a hospital. This is a profession to which many are invited but most wisely reject.

The exception to my harsh rule is a good mother. Most willingly nurse their babies; many spend their subsequent existences attending to the needs of their offspring. Without a mother, the orphan wanders in limbo.

O

O is sublimely beautiful because it has no starting or ending point. Unlike human lives circumscribed by a beginning and an end, O, like great works of art, evades time's net. Definitely Shakespeare's favourite letter: "O brave new world," "O that this too too solid flesh would melt."

OBSERVATION: As in "under observation." Not until my third week in Shanghai did Mr. Sanders' brother-in-law put in an appearance. Strangely, he visited me at home quite late one night. Since this fellow spoke only Chinese, I went to my bedroom, retrieved the gift and knocked on Chang's bedroom door. Although obviously awoken from a sound sleep, he dressed quickly, greeted our visitor and began his work as interpreter.

The brother-in-law did not stay long. Exceptionally tall for a Chinese and dressed in simple worker's clothes, his long, lean face wore a worried expression. He gratefully received his brother-in-law's gift. Could he possibly prevail upon me to carry back to Canada a gift for Mr. and Mrs. Sanders? I agreed, whereupon he told me that he would convey it to me as soon as he could. With that assurance, he took his leave.

By the outset of my final week in Shanghai, Mr. Sanders' brother-in-law had not put in another appearance. I wondered if, perhaps, he and his wife had not found a suitable gift. Much more concerned with completing my work and getting ready for my departure, I thought no more of the matter.

On the Thursday before my departure, again late at night, this fellow reappeared. He carried with him a parcel that looked exactly like the one I had given to him. I was about to accept the package when the front door of the house burst open. Suddenly, a dozen policemen surrounded us. They threw Mr. Sanders' brother-in-law to the floor, seized the parcel, told Chang and myself to be seated, and then half-a-dozen of them ran into my bedroom, where I heard the noise of breaking glass and hurled objects. They rummaged around before joining their comrades in the sitting room.

The police informed Chang and me that the parcel contained an antique statue of Buddha of inestimable value. I had inadvertently carried a replica of it into China. Two days after I had given Mr. Sanders' gift to his brother-in-law, the real thing had been taken from a temple in Nanjing and the fake inserted as a replacement. This kind of robbery — the equivalent Chinese word is in English "a sting" — had been carried out in broad daylight. An accomplice had positioned himself near the statue, cried out loudly that a pickpocket had stolen his wallet, and diverted the attention of passersby, whereupon the thief brazenly snatched the Buddha and substituted the replica in its place. This scam might have been successful but for the observant eyes of a ten-year-old boy who witnessed the event and informed his father of what he had beheld.

Unawares, I would have carried the genuine object back to Canada, where the fake had been manufactured by Mr. Sanders' wife, who worked as a "restorer" in the Far Eastern department at the Royal Ontario Museum. Evidently, the Sanders had intended to peddle the real Buddha to the institution where she was employed.

The police also told Chang that I was not under suspicion of any crime, but they had been instructed to search my room thoroughly. At that point, with the criminal in chains, they left us in peace. When I returned to my bedroom, I discovered that my camera lay in ruins on the floor, that my negatives and prints had been confiscated, and that my clothing was strewn all about.

Chang was in tears. After retrieving the Hasselblad from the floor, he promised to recover the negatives and photographs. Of course, that proved to be an impossible task. My work had disappeared. I lamented its loss but not as poignantly as my friend did.

When I arrived back in Canada a few days later, I learned that Mr. Sanders had been detained by the RCMP and was no longer an employee of the Royal Bank.

At the airport, Chang embraced me and promised to stay in

touch. He told me that I could send him letters by way of the Royal but that I must not refer to political issues in any missive. He would find a way of contacting me. The future was not bright for someone like himself. "I think too much; Chairman Mao does not like such people."

OBSERVE: Before travelling to China, although I had spent part of every Saturday at the Toronto Public Library, I seldom borrowed books. Now I searched a wide variety — especially those on China, on Buddhism, on Karl Marx — and borrowed them. I stopped watching television in the evening and read instead. In this way, I would get through four or five books a week.

Then, in a curious change, I started borrowing books on the history of art, Western and non-Western. I became fascinated by the relationship between patronage and the life of the often struggling artists. I deeply admired those men and women who had never received any kind of genuine recognition. I came to admire even more the rootless, wandering, unhappy Vincent van Gogh. I esteemed even more his brother Theo for the unconditional love he bestowed on his difficult, irascible sibling.

To this day I do not know why — a month after I arrived home — I walked into Brown's, the art supply shop, and purchased twenty pieces of art paper, colour pencils and two books on how to draw. My first efforts badly disappointed me. I threw all the early drawings away, returned to the supply shop the following week, bought forty sheets of paper, reread the two manuals and started anew.

Ever since I began taking photographs and, then, drawing, I see better. I do not mean that there has been any kind of physical improvement in my eyesight, but my "immodest" eyes are always looking about, anxious to consume everything they see as if no opportunity is to be missed.

If my tongue remains blocked from the expression of my feelings, perhaps my eyes might not be so impaired. I might possess "a good eye."

Outwardly, my life has not changed. Of course, I fretted the loss of the camera and the photographs. Would photography have provided me with the opportunity to alter my previous existence? I did not know the response to that question, but I had no inclination to find an answer by taking new pictures. Most of all, I became anxious about another person — a new experience for me: I worried constantly about Chang. What would happen to him?

At work, everyone was obviously aware of what had happened; no one cross-questioned me. I was simply welcomed back. The new manager, Mrs. Nicholson, was brusque, but usually pleasant.

ONGOING: As soon as I boarded the plane in Shanghai — and throughout the three long flights that deposited me back in Toronto — I thought of all the things I could have said in response to Chang's queries. All the questions I should have asked crystallized. My only consolation is that I have never been able — despite mighty efforts — to force my mouth to utter my real feelings to anyone. For instance, I had never told Madame Beaulieu that I loved her; in addition, I had never acknowledged in words the great debt I owed her. Whenever the impulse to declare such emotions surfaced, my tongue refused to obey me.

Squirmed into the confined spaces of the various aircraft, I became consumed by what were, for me, familiar twin feelings: anger and frustration. Accompanying these unhappy sensations was the loss of the photographs. Of the camera I was not unduly concerned: it had been destroyed and that was that. The lost photos were not of the quality that Chang claimed — of that I was very sure.

OPTIMIST: Guardedly, I could use this noun to describe myself. Why is that? I suspect is it because I have been around Madame Beaulieu for so long. Her strong feelings about the existence of goodness are contagious.

ORANGE RIVER: The longest river in South Africa. I often think of that country as a deeply unhappy place, and I know that South Africa was once the Orange Free State. Yet the image of an orange-coloured river lined with lush, beautiful, blossoming trees moves me.

ORDER: I have lost my hold on it ever since I began the drawings. I suspect I am writing this diary to restore a semblance of it to my now chaotic life.

ORDINARY: The return to normality. Since I arrived back on schedule and seemed none the worse for the experience, I volunteered no information about the fate of my camera. The three boys were delighted with the toys I had purchased for them; the adult Beaulieus enthusiastically praised the large cloisonné bowl adorned with pink and red chrysanthemums I had obtained for them in a market stall at one-third the asking price. Chang had bargained on my behalf. He had responded with disgust to the asking price, which was immediately cut in half. When he tried to whittle that down, the vendor was recalcitrant. Chang nodded at me, screamed at the dealer and informed me that we would be on our way. We had walked no more than five steps when the seller ran after us and offered the bowl at a now drastically reduced price.

That evening Madame Beaulieu walked up to my room. What had gone wrong? she asked. Without fail, she always knows when I am troubled. She seemed neither dismayed nor shocked. "It is the way of the world. Such horrible things occur more frequently than we would like. You must purchase another camera."

ORIENTEERING: If this sport were added to the school curriculum, would it provide students with a useful model of how to conduct their lives? In my experience, destinations are not only elusive but invisible.

ORPHAN: In typesetting, the first line of a paragraph at the foot of a page.

Chang once advised me, "An orphan has a very special opportunity not allowed to those with parents. He can be the author of his own destiny. He does not have parents looking over his shoulder at every opportunity, ready to encourage or discourage. My grandparents, who raised me, were simply too old to make any effort to form me. For better of worse, I am truly a self-manufactured person. You must do the same with your existence."

ORPHEUS: A great but doomed artist. A man madly in love with his dead wife; he could not keep his eyes off her. By definition, the artist must always, even at his peril, be an avid observer.

OSMOSIS: What did I assimilate in order to become an artist?

Nine years after I began my strange enterprise in 1958, I have an enormous cache of work. I still have no idea today in 1967 — when my output has reached 1,112 illustrations — whether my work has any merit. No one else has seen it. I am hesitant to tell anyone that I have a secret life. I obviously do not wish to become a laughing-stock. Only Madame Beaulieu would understand and mutter sympathetic encouragement.

"If these drawings are going to remain hidden," I asked myself, "why do I bother to do them? An artist, after all, needs an audience." I still cannot answer that query.

Of one thing I soon became certain. When I made the drawings, I was no longer Étienne the Orphan or Étienne the Bank Teller or Étienne the Silent. For a while, I became Étienne Who Had Gone on the Mysterious Trip to China. Then, suddenly, I began to think of myself as Étienne the Artist.

The difficulty was that I did not know this person, such a vastly different reincarnation was he of my old self. This new man became preoccupied with his drawings — more accurately, he was obsessed. He thought of them all the time. He may not have made any mistakes at the Bank in taking in or dispensing money, but his mind was elsewhere.

Madame Beaulieu was surprised that he no longer had time for *I Love Lucy* on Monday nights: "You were so much in love with her," she playfully admonished him. My landlady may have been unfailingly pleasant to this new person, but I came to detest him. He was inordinately ambitious. He was ruthless. He was a creature guilty of the sin of pride, the worst of the seven deadly sins.

The only person to whom the new Étienne could confess his newfound ambitions was Chang, seven thousand miles away. He wrote him many times, realizing that those letters were probably either lost or confiscated. He did have the hope that Chang could become, in the manner of a Theo van Gogh, a sounding board.

Étienne the Artist cares more about empathy than he would like to admit: he is not drawing and painting merely for his own benefit.

OUTREACH: In November 1958, I wrote to Chang. How is it that I, who am so hopelessly tongue-tied in conversation, have all of a sudden found a voice in which to write?

I was infused with energy after I returned from China. In place of my woebegotten ambition to become another Cartier-Bresson, I purchased a wide assortment of coloured pencils and paper at an art-supply store.

I had no idea what I hoped to accomplish. I did, however, much to my amazement, begin a series of drawings. In order to remind myself that such an activity was to help me loosen my tongue, I linked each to a letter from the alphabet. I suppose I became very much like a small boy eagerly going from letter to letter in an alphabet book, except that I was the adult constructing the book.

I told Chang he was my audience for these drawings. How I yearned to send some to him. Perhaps they best express the language of my heart, although they are only of simple things: still lifes with fruits and vegetables arranged to look as if carelessly tossed together, small chairs placed near creaky old beds, some views of Toronto. They are not the stuff of real art, but they are the closest I can come to a grammar of feeling. If you eventually see these small efforts, I asked him, perhaps each one will be worth the thousand words I was never able to utter when we were together.

OVERDUE: On December 4, 1960, a long-awaited letter reached me from Chang. He had attempted to write me earlier, but he suspected his efforts had been in vain. A friend who had gone on business to Paris mailed the missive to me.

My letters made him gasp. All my reticence in conversation had vanished. I seemed a different person. "Why can't you speak as you write?" he asked. Maybe my true self was only revealed when I put pen to paper.

A month after I left Shanghai, he was dismissed from his job. He was cast adrift, thrown out of the walls of commerce. He worked briefly in a bicycle factory, where he assembled sprockets, his salary reduced to ten per cent of what he had previously earned. Then came another change. He was sent to the countryside for "retraining."

He and his new comrades were deposited at a remote railway station in the north. They marched for two days — choked and bruised in stifling air. The village to which they were assigned was a poverty-stricken, flea-infested place where they assisted the peasants in constructing a dam. The dampness multiplied the efforts of mosquitoes to eat all of the newcomers alive: his body was so covered with welts that he could not call it his own.

He could no longer express a real opinion. If he uttered the slightest word of criticism, he would be thrown into prison. If the opportunity arose, he would smuggle another letter out.

That letter reached me three years after my departure from Shanghai! My work on my drawings continued, although I very much wanted the solace of discussing my new life with Chang.

At night I dreamt that terrible misfortunes overtook him, but soon, the nightmares took a strange twist. I would be abandoned in a terror-filled foreign city — Paris, Berlin, Shanghai — pursued by gun-toting, drug-dealing gangsters whose nefarious activities I had been on the verge of exposing. I would be surrounded by a swarm of these mobsters in a deserted warehouse, about to meet my end, when all of a sudden a mysterious presence would make itself known. My tormentors would look around, become flustered and vanish. My rescuer was Chang, who I embraced in gratitude.

Only after I endured this dream half a dozen times did it occur to me that Tintin had been saved by his friend Chang in *Le Lotus bleu* whereas the reporter had returned the favour in *Tintin au Tibet*. If life could only be as easy as fiction.

OVERJOYED: I am a bit reluctant to put this down in the event I bring bad luck raining down on me, but the sheer pleasure I experience when making my drawings elates me. Not so when writing, when I have to measure every word I expend.

OVERLOAD: This word relates to the previous entry. I often feel that my sensorium becomes so glutted when I draw that my entire self — body and soul — is electrified. Sometimes I wonder if I am well on my way to becoming a complete lunatic.

P is a narrow letter puffing itself up grandiosely because it begins ten per cent of all the words in the English language. It is also a bit of a dandy, insisting that proper reverence be paid to its appearance. It aspires to be a gentleman or gentlewoman, but it is only concerned with the shape of its bowl — and not to the inner life the opening represents. This letter displays the triumph of form over substance.

PACE: For what seemed like an eternity, Time marched slowly forward. Each day of the week was a precise measure that I could rely on: five days of work, two of rest. After my trip to China, I have not been able to return to normality.

Rather indulgently, Time once spread itself out lazily in front of me. Now I have to plan every moment and, despite my best efforts, I can never have enough Time to accomplish what I wish. The truth is that Time has become an enemy, scurrying forward relentlessly and devouring everything in its path. I must do my job at the Bank properly for forty hours a week, but then I have to salvage all the Time I can for the drawings.

PARENTS: I hardly ever think of my birth parents. Are they odd like me? Are they still alive? Why did my mother abandon me? These questions come whizzing in every so often. I do not like to deal with such speculations. Would answers to any of these questions be of any conceivable value? I always respond with disinterest when such queries — arising in my uncon-scious — present themselves. They are best pushed under the carpet.

What good would it do for me to know that my birth mother reluctantly left me at the Orphanage? What kind of relation-ship could I have with a person who treated me so cruelly? As to my father, I am sure he was a real brute, a first-class bully. Perhaps he raped my mother.

Some days, my sentimental side asserts itself despite my best efforts to keep it at bay. On such occasions, I can think of all kinds of mitigating circumstances that led to my abandon-ment. My mother and father were too poor to keep a child; my mother wept mightily when she left me in the care of the nuns.

PASCAL, BLAISE: The supreme master of the aphorism — the perfect literary form to capture the fluctuations of the human mind. A reclusive and compulsive eccentric, he had some sort of internal thermometer that allowed him to monitor the workings of his tormented soul with a great deal of precision.

PATIENCE: Madame Beaulieu thinks one can never possess too much of this spiritual commodity. She certainly has plenty to bestow on me. I have sometimes wondered if Tante Isabelle might bankrupt her sister's supply.

PATRIOTISM: Am I truly Canadian — despite all the hoopla in the press about Confederation?

All three of the Beaulieu children are good cases in point on this issue. Only fourteen-year-old Paul still lives here in 1967, although the other two visit as often as they can. Luc is twenty; Jean-Pierre eighteen. Neither of them ever liked school. Madame thinks they were slow learners in large part because their teachers were put off by the fact that they spoke English with heavy French accents. "Our fault," Madame observes. "We should not have insisted that they speak French at home. A terrible mistake."

For whatever reason, the two left school in their middle teens, obtained low-paying factory work and were miserable. Luc went west to find work in construction, but he could not adjust to the Prairies. Unemployment was high in Quebec and so he did not emigrate there. Having heard that there were pockets of French-Canadians in New England, he went there to investigate.

Within two weeks of arriving, he wrote his mother to say he felt completely at home. The place he had had settled in

— Willimantic, Connecticut — was predominantly French-speaking, having been established by émigrés from la belle province. He had never felt so at home in his life, he informed her. French-Canadians were the norm — not the miserable exception — in this small American city. Within six months, Jean-Pierre followed hid elder brother's lead and now lives in Woonsocket, Rhode Island. Paul is vowing to join his brothers when he turns eighteen.

How can there be a Canada for those who speak French if we can only live in Quebec and some exceedingly small pockets in the other provinces? How can the Beaulieu brothers be Canadian if they are forced to settle in New England in order to feel a measure of freedom from discrimination?

PERMUTATIONS: The extraordinary letter was enclosed in an envelope mailed from somewhere in Toronto and had the most beautiful Japanese stamp of a pink chrysanthemum on it. I have translated it from French into English. It is dated March 18, 1965.

My dearest Étienne,

You will be astounded by the adjective I have used in my salutation. You may well reject my entitlement to use it. In any event, you will be startled to receive a letter from the woman who gave birth to you thirty-three years ago. I do not call myself your mother because I am not worthy of that name. I abandoned you within the first few hours after you were born and have no right to a designation that correctly belongs to women who look after their offspring. I am writing to implore your understanding and, certainly, your forgiveness.

I am in my fiftieth year and full of shame and guilt at the way I treated you. For the past five years I have debated with myself as to whether I should attempt to get in touch. Perhaps my little boy is best left to his own devices, my dark side asserts. But he was left at the door of an orphanage. Perhaps he needs your assistance — that is what my good side tells me.

After much debate, I approached the order of nuns — the Loretto Sisters — who ran the now long-closed orphanage at the door of which I placed your shivering little body. My phone calls and letters went unanswered and so I presented myself at the mother house a year ago when I was briefly back in Canada. I explained the purpose of my visit to the sister who answered the door. "The information you request is not available under any circumstances. Besides, the infant you left in our care might not have survived. There is nothing to be done."

My onslaught of tears embarrassed the poor woman, who was obviously not used to dealing with lunatics. She handed me a box of Kleenex and informed me that she would ask someone else to speak with me. I collected myself as best I could and waited impatiently for another nun to put in an appearance.

The woman who entered the room a half hour later was well into her nineties I suspect. I stood to receive her, but she told me to be seated. Large she may be, but she has a touch of elegance in her carriage and manner. Although I could see steely grey eyes, a hawk-like nose and a thin mouth, she seemed a kind person.

"Why do you think the infant you abandoned survived?"

"I know he did. The day after I left him I saw a short piece in the newspaper stating that a baby boy had been abandoned at the Orphanage. The report stated that he was small — barely five pounds — but in excellent health."

"You obviously were concerned about the infant if you consulted the newspaper."

"Yes. I felt that I had done a wicked thing in leaving him."

She changed the subject. "We are not supposed to reunite foundlings with their parents. It is forbidden."

"I wish to know only that he is still alive and in good health."

Since Mother Clothilde's terse manner indicated to me that she wanted to know more about me before revealing the merest glimmer of information, I told her about the circumstances leading up to your birth. I assured her that I came from a middle-class family from the NDG area of Montreal, that I had been inexperienced sexually when, at the age of sixteen at summer camp in Cornwall, I met a boy one year older than me from Toronto, that I had intercourse with him once and that I subsequently became pregnant. Throughout my pregnancy I did not gain much weight.

In fact, I gave birth to you by myself in an alleyway about four blocks from the Orphanage. I was in shock due to the blood and the pain, but I struggled to my feet for what seemed like an eternity. By looking at my watch, I guessed that four hours had passed. I knew of the existence of the Orphanage and thus wandered in its direction in order to leave you behind.

The nun did not appear unduly startled by my confession. Had I subsequently been in touch with the father? Yes. I told her. We had exchanged letters later that summer and autumn. Then, I heard nothing. I wanted to discuss my pregnancy with him. In desperation, I telephoned his home in Toronto. Mrs. Donnelly answered the phone. When I asked to speak with her son, she seemed to swoon on the other end of the line. "Bobby died suddenly in his sleep two weeks ago. The doctors said he had an undiagnosed heart ailment. He was snatched away from us." There was a long pause. At the other end of the line, Mrs. Donnelly was obviously trying to restore herself to a semblance of normality. "Were you a friend of his?" I explained that I had met him at camp that summer. I told her that I was sorry for her loss and put the phone down as soon as I could.

The nun looked at me intently. "So your little boy was half-French, half-English?" I nodded in assent. After what seemed like an eternity, the sister told me that your given name — chosen by her — was Étienne. "I remember him well. A very good, although unusual boy. I should not do this, but if you wish to write him a letter, I am fairly certain I can get it to him."

This letter has been a long time in composition. I returned to Tokyo, where I now live. Having taken no responsibility for your existence, I hesitated to interfere with your life. I began letter after letter and found them all unsatisfactory. They read like the outpourings of a demented, guilt-ridden person. Such missives would merely underscore your conviction that your mother was a completely hopeless human being, one unworthy of either respect or love.

With much trepidation, I am finally able to complete a letter. If Sister is as good as her word, you may get to read the outpourings of a distraught parent. Please write me. Despite the years of neglect, I am your loving and devoted mother,

Beatrice

That letter went unanswered for a long time. I was stunned but not moved. I did not want anything to do with this strange woman, a wayward teenager who had carried me for nine months and then left me in someone's doorway.

Three weeks after receiving the missive, I showed it to Madame Beaulieu. To my surprise, she burst into tears when she read it. "This letter was composed by a very loving, generous person, Étienne. She feels deeply ashamed of what she did and loves the infant to whom she gave birth." My landlady searched my face to see if I was taking in what she was saying. She was looking for anger, but she found only incomprehension. "Think about what this good lady has revealed, Étienne. Consider her suffering."

Only after reflecting on Madame Beaulieu's advice for well over a month did I pen a short letter to my mother in Japan. I could not really tell her anything about myself — I somehow felt unable to do so. Instead, I summarized the barest of facts and requested that she provide me with more information about herself, as if I were putting her on trial.

PHOTOGRAPHY: A wonderful way of telling lies. I remain a journeyman in that art. The world looks vastly different when framed by the rectangle of a camera lens. As I walked about Shanghai, I was continually amazed at how a temple would be dramatically transformed as soon as the camera gave it a shape. The camera creates an untruth when it sets a building apart from its surroundings, robbing it of a context. Yet, quite often, a temple that first appeared to be merely another uninteresting part of a shabby neighbourhood gained nobility when shown to better advantage by itself.

For a week I had been passing by the greengrocer on the corner of the street where we lived. Then I asked the proprietor if I might photograph the wares on sale. He nodded in agreement after I showed the camera to him. As I prepared to take my shots, I observed the humdrum objects as if I had never seen their likes before.

For instance, there were the leeks. The paper-thin, heavily veined crinkly green and yellow leaves that encased this vegetable were something I had never paid attention to before.

Was I continuing in a relentless pursuit of superficiality? Or was I looking more intently at the surfaces of things? I remained a person without a firm metaphysics.

PICASSO: His ruthlessness attracts and repels me. How could he ever have thought it was his right to treat others so callously? Other peoples' lives were mere grist for his mill. Those beautiful Madonnas look down adoringly at their babies, admiring their own cleverness at having produced such handsome offspring. The infants are filled with a sense of complete well-being — they are the most beautiful creatures in the universe. And then there are the canvases in which the poor, maimed and suffering parade their woes before the viewer.

Picasso the man was cruel, violent, selfish and vindictive. He took all the beauty he could find, put it on canvas and was himself devoid of human feelings. To paint, say, compassion, he obviously had to strip himself of that emotion.

Poor Vincent van Gogh was also a megalomaniac but of a somewhat gentler kind. He was irritable, tetchy, and more than a little vain. Unlike Picasso, he turned his inward eye against himself.

The sad truth is that all artists are miscreants. Their eyes tell them too much; they spend their time putting what they behold on canvas or paper; they have precious little left for their own lives.

In some ways I am fortunate. I have always been solitary and have little or no inclination to impose what I see on others. My art will always be a completely private one.

POLYPHONIC: The stirring, contrapuntal music of the Middle Ages. So far my diary has been in one voice, and I am not sure I wish to cede control to others by allowing them to speak.

PRESENT: For most people there is only one reality. "I never think about yesterday," a colleague once informed me: "Even if it is a pleasant memory, it's gone. Only today matters," he added. That person, without being aware of it, shares the sentiments of Henry Ford: "History is bunk."

If that's what most people think — it's not what they feel. Paul McCartney has it right: the grim present is here to stay. In the gospel according to Étienne, in the crumbled ruins of the past — to mix my metaphors shamelessly — reside the seeds of salvation.

PRIDE: As mentioned earlier, the Chief of the Seven Deadly Sins. I now became his prisoner. The first series of drawings were of household objects: chairs, tables, ironing boards, glasses, vases, shirts, pillowcases. Why I felt compelled to inscribe a G onto a rendition of a drinking glass, I have no definitive idea. Perhaps I wanted the plainness of the subject depicted to be contrasted to the inventiveness bestowed upon the curlicues of the G? Having set down that path, I could not turn back. Every drawing had to be labelled with a letter of the alphabet. There was no other way for me. I would have been unable to continue had I not followed that simple, compelling rule.

Perhaps I am a person who must always exert control in some form or other. Not really satisfied in my choice of the hidden life of the artist, did I need to use letters to comfort myself that I was not merely succumbing to a messy existence?

On Saturday afternoons I spend a great deal of time at the Art Gallery of Toronto, recently rechristened the Art Gallery of Ontario. The guards know me well. I am one of those hangers-on they treat as harmless eccentrics. Some of them smile at me; some act as if I do not exist.

The commercial galleries are a different story. Usually the owners are not there. A young, thin, blond woman reading Jack Kerouac sits at the back of one of them — she has been reading *On the Road* for three months. Once, in an attempt to converse with her, I pointed out that Kerouac came from a

French-Canadian family who lived in the States. She looked at me quizzically. When I asked her for some information about the artist whose work I was looking at, she pointed to some clippings on a small glass coffee table at the front of the gallery. She has even less words at her command than I.

I remained undeterred by ignorance — my own or that of others. From domestic subjects, I moved to cityscapes and landscapes. My knowledge of Toronto and Shanghai was of limited use because I was fascinated with interior landscapes: places that could exist only in my imagination. I ransacked my dreams and nightmares for inspiration; I scoured art books: Klee, Brueghel, Paul Nash, Edward Burra, Klimt, Balthus, Toulouse-Lautrec and "Le Douanier" Rousseau were particularly generous to a young whippersnapper. Then came the animals. Like Noah, I attempted to capture every bird and animal that ever existed.

I've painted a limited number of portraits. I lack the nerve to render what Blake calls the "human form divine." Becoming an artist may have made me into a monumental egotist, but I knew from the outset that I lacked the wherewithal to capture a smile or a frown. The reality of a nose, a mouth, a dimple, or an eye would always find a way to evade me. I surrendered to this fact, to the knowledge that I could never know another person well enough to draw them. Even Madame Beaulieu, whom I adore, is out of my extremely limited range. Although I see her every day, I have made unsatisfactory portraits of her. I cannot quite capture the soft tenderness that animates her face.

PROFANE: If you attend to the profane, the sacred will take care of itself. My drawings have taught me this lesson. If I infuse my creatures with sufficient life, they will of necessity have a religious aura to them, so connected will they be to the essential mysteries of the universe. If I could but make profane representations of Madame Beaulieu, they would be successful. I am trying, against my own best advice, to make them sacred.

Q

Q preens itself on its separateness from all the other letters. Is it merely an **O** with a little curlicue added? Or is its entire raison d'être in that tiny jaunty bow tie? This letter is also inimical to all other letters in the formation of English words except **U**, which it obviously sees as a kindred spirit.

QUANDARY: A good word to describe life: an extended series of unanswered, unanswerable questions.

For me, Time has become my biggest concern. Time, I know to my cost, is a savage master, who would devour me whole.

QUILTS: I stand in awe when I behold the ways in which the Amish women construct their masterpieces from dross. An old piece of dungaree, a discarded washcloth, a worn-out towel.

These remnants are then sewn together. Sometimes the resulting patterns resemble familiar things such as log cabins; sometimes the patterns are abstract. No matter what they decide to make, their creations come beautifully and forcefully together.

QUIXOTIC: A word that I cannot apply to myself. For years I have wondered about the lives of my parents and now that the opportunity has presented itself to be reunited with one of them, I am hesitant. I entertain no chivalrous feelings towards my mother.

The possibility of receiving love, even admiration, confuses and distresses me. When the second letter from Japan reached me, I waited almost a week before opening it. Would it tell me things I did not really want to know? Would it provide me with any sense of satisfaction or pleasure? "You've become a very hard-hearted person, Étienne," I told myself.

Perhaps, I wondered, I do not wish to subject myself to disappointment and a further rejection? On the other hand, what would be my mother's reaction when she discovered the true nature of the strange, unsociable excuse for a son she had produced? Would she be repulsed? Or would she blame herself for having given life to a misfit? With a great deal of trepidation, I wrote her a brief note.

My mother's second letter began with an elaborate autobiographical summary. Since she remained slender throughout her pregnancy and wore some full-fitting skirts in the final two months, she evaded detection by her parents, her teachers and her schoolmates. She confided not a word to a single soul.

After giving birth to me and depositing me at the Orphanage, she returned home, snuck by her parents, retreated to her bedroom and then took a warm bath. She then informed her parents she was coming down with a bad cold and would retire for the night. Only in the dark stillness of her bedroom did she cry herself to sleep.

February 1, 1966

Dearest Étienne,

I feel that I must still address you as "dearest" although your letter gives me little hope that you shall ever apply even the adjective "dear" to me. I also thought you might ask why my letter was sent from Japan. You have asked me few questions about myself. I thought you might be curious about me. I had told myself that you would be full of questions about me and my subsequent existence. Instead, you have inquired about my reasons for contacting you. You have not implied any sinister design on my part. I have no right to hurt feelings, I tell myself repeatedly, but that reminder is of little help in this instance. I am in fear and trembling as I write.

After I left you, I redoubled my efforts to be a dutiful daughter to my father. My sweet and gentle mother never made any demands. She liked me just as I was. Not so Father. He had determined that I must be a great success in the eyes of the world in order to have any chance of gaining his approval. From the time I was very young, he impressed upon me the fact that a francophone's only genuine measure of self-esteem was one found in the admiration of a highly placed

English speaker. If admiration was not forthcoming, one's
efforts were in vain. There was one way round this dilemma:
if one challenged and then surpassed an anglophone, that was
perhaps better than obtaining admiration.

My father, who worked as a clerk in the men's clothing
department at Ogilvy's on Ste. Catherine's Street, spoke perfect
English. However, his mastery of his second language was very
much that of an overly mannered servant whose deportment
and manners exceed his master's. In fact, my father's
command of his second language was so exact that it placed
all his customers at a disadvantage because their own agility
in their native language lagged below his. Occasionally, a
befuddled Captain of Industry — certain that my father
was having fun at his expense — would complain to the
department head that Monsieur Ambrose was somehow
making fun of him. My father once overheard someone
observe, "That fellow is taking the piss out of me!" Of course,
Father assured his boss that such was not the case, but I
think he took a guilty pleasure in this encounter. Like all
slaves, he did not mind rebelling, however gently, against
an oppressor.

I was sixteen when I gave birth to you in 1932. Although
I considered myself very fortunate in having given birth in
complete secrecy, I paid a high price. I felt guilty about
abandoning a helpless infant. I thought of you constantly.
How will he celebrate today? I asked myself on the morning
of your third birthday. How well does he speak? I pondered
when you were four. Is he a good student? Is he well taken
care of by the nuns?

Coupled with those concerns, I felt I had to be the daughter my father insisted I be. Book learning came easily to me. Since I was good in all subjects, my father decided I should become a doctor rather than a teacher. For a while, he had considered the latter as a career path but, upon the advice of his cronies, he told me that I must pursue medicine. "McGill, I am told, has one of the finest medical schools in the world. Its doors are not easily opened to us Quebecers — or to women. You will break down that gate. Of that, my dear girl, I have no doubt."

Of course, Father was correct. I entered pre-med at McGill directly from high school, did very well and was a doctor by the time I was twenty-four. Then there was the question of a specialty. Father had (pardon the pun!) his heart set on Cardiology, but I finally allowed myself the luxury of a small rebellion. I did not care for such work, I informed my vexed parent: I did not wish to be a surgeon, nor was I willing to spend all my time as a diagnostician. "What does suit you, then? he asked politely, hiding as much as possible his disap-pointment. I informed him that I was tempted by the fairly new science of Radiology, which allowed physicians to look at x-rays to help determine the underlying causes of disease.

My father was not pleased. He thought that I was making my choice with the misguided notion that my life should be devoted to helping others! When I pointed out to him that was exactly what a doctor was supposed to do with her life, he was furious. Successful physicians pursued one of two career paths: there were those like Madame Curie who gave their lives to the service of science and became celebrities; then there were those who treated famous patients and became rich, and whose photographs often appeared in the newspapers.

Radiology was a new, largely unproven branch of Medicine. It was, according to my father, an Ugly Duckling of a specialty. When I pointed out to Father that the Ugly Duckling had eventually been transformed into a beautiful Swan, he threw up his hands in disgust.

Strange as it may seem, this was my supreme act of resistance against my demanding father. For more than ten years I had been attempting to balance my filial obligation to Father and my increasing sense that I had to lead a life of service, even sacrifice. How, otherwise, I asked myself, could I possibly make up for my cowardly behaviour in abandoning my little boy? Those were the twin poles in my existence: duty and guilt. That unsavoury combination dominated me. I had no social life, no friends. Having made up my mind, I did indeed become a Radiologist, saw my father less frequently than before (I had to sneak home to visit with Maman) and then made the decision in 1945 to emigrate to Japan. I shall tell you what followed the next time I write.

Beatrice

QUOTIDIAN. So many of the days of our life are filled with sorrow and disappointment. I have composed another letter I cannot mail. I told Chang that I endured nightmares in which horrible things overtook him. I assured him my drawings continued at a furious pace. I told him that I was preoccupied by the letter I had received from my birth mother and that she lived in Japan. Her letters, I admitted to him, were filled with tenderness. I did not intend to respond, but Madame Beaulieu suggested I do so: "A son belongs with his mother," she admonished me.

My heart remained closed to this possibility until I recollected that he and I, who had known each other for only a short period of time, had forged a strong bond. Perhaps, after all these years, I told him, I can come to some knowledge of the being who gave me life. She is a physician and, I am sure, a person who endeavours to practise charity. My heart is now open to her. Will we, at long last, be reunited? What did he think of this strange event?

We humans are such strange, contradictory creatures, I reminded him. What gives us sorrow also gives us happiness. That is the paradox we would rather be ignorant of since it is so much easier to experience only one emotion at a time. Who wants to feel sorrow, joy, anger and contentment simultaneously? We are ill-equipped for such demands on our frail mental systems.

"Your well-being preoccupies much of my time," I confessed to him. "Will we ever see each other again?" I asked. "When I think of you, I am so flooded by such a wide variety of emotions — happiness, loss, love — that I sometimes think I shall perish."

R

R has a complex inner life. Its bowl is its pride and joy. Unlike P and B, all self-respecting Rs insist that this part of itself requires careful attention.

RADIO: The Beaulieus and I eagerly listened before television took over our lives. I did not enjoy the cop-and-robber serials and the fare usually enjoyed by young people. Instead, I looked forward to Sunday evenings when Jack Benny, his beloved Mary Livingstone, and his valet, Rochester, enacted their various domestic squabbles. Jack was a creature of many sides. He loved playing the violin, although he was supremely untalented at it (it was a security blanket); he was also a determined miser, who spent his pennies twice. So why did I like him? Despite his extreme narcissism, Benny made fun of himself — and he was only a bit angry when others pointed out to him his many frailties. He always claimed to be 39, but he offered that claim half-heartedly.

From him I think I first gained a sense of self-irony. No one is as important as they would like to be.

RASCALLY: No one would have applied this adjective to Étienne the child or teenager. Now I am a bit underhanded. Some days I feel mischievous, even frisky. I have become a bit secretive even with Madame B. I have not revealed even to her my secret life as an artist. She would approve and congratulate me — that goes without saying. Yet I cannot bear to tell her. I want something that is only mine.

RATS: Like wolves, creatures not liked by most people. These rodents are associated with filthy sewers, slums, and rotting garbage. A person who is a "rat" is someone who acts badly, usually by betraying a friend.

When I was six years old, one of my compatriots, who bore the strange name of Homer, was given a white rat by a visitor, a farmer uncle. When he asked what name he should give the animal, I suggested Virgil. For two days, we kept the existence of the poetic rat from the nuns. Virgil was quite happy in the shoebox in which he lived, and he was grateful for the small remnants from our meals with which we fed him. In fact, Virgil was a beautiful sleek and white animal. If nature had given him a human incarnation, he would have been a dexterous, prize-winning athlete.

Unfortunately, Homer could not keep a secret. He was certain that Sister Maurice, of whom he was very fond, would share his affection for the animal. When she entered our room, intrigued by Homer's assertion that he had something wonderful to show her, she could hardly contain her expectation of seeing a wondrous sight. Her screams could be heard the length and breadth of the Orphanage. Mother Clothilde was asked to deal with the crisis. In her no-nonsense way she marched into our quarters, opened the box, and smiled broadly. She looked at the two of us as we quaked in apprehension. "He is a beautiful creature — look at the way his little pink nose twitches as he tries to figure everything out! There is no doubt that you should love him, boys, but he does not belong within our walls. It is not natural for him to live indoors. This evening, after dark, we will set him free." The three of us were in tears when we returned from our mission. Most commonplace assumptions do not stand up when tested by reality.

REAR WINDOW: I went to see it when it first came out about ten years ago. I was looking forward to the usual elaborate cat-and-mouse game with which Hitchcock teases his audience.

We are supposed to like Jimmy Stewart in any of his cinematic incarnations as the American everyman, but I was a bit dubious from the outset that a woman as enchanting as Grace Kelly would be chasing him, instead of the other way around! Jimmy was irascible, difficult to please — a real curmudgeon. And there was this beautiful creature trying to please him! I could not suspend my disbelief. I even had mixed feelings when Raymond Burr tried to kill Jimmy. A part of me wanted the villain to succeed.

Those were initial reactions. A week later, Jimmy began appearing in my dreams. He would come to my wicket at the bank, explain that he had been away for a while because of an accident and, in his usual pleasant manner, make a withdrawal. For a while, that was it. Then, he was in my room looking out my window, binoculars in hand. That was deeply annoying. I had not given him permission to enter my room. He nodded sagely in my direction but acted as if I were invisible. What would the Beaulieus think if they found out that someone was spying on the neighbours in back of us? I'd order him out of my room. He always seemed to be about to say something in his customary drawl, think better of it, shrug his shoulders and vanish.

Then Jimmy disappeared. In the new dreams, binoculars in hand, I was the peeping Tom. I then became terrified the Beaulieus might evict me if they found out what I was doing. I awoke from these encounters in a cold sweat. I was relieved to return to reality, but I wondered what I could possibly have been looking for.

REINCARNATION: Catholicism's belief in an afterlife assures the faithful that they will somehow be reconstituted after death. The myth reassures the believer that existence in that new sphere will be both the same and yet infinitely better. I must have been four when one of the nuns referred to the Buddhist belief in reincarnation wherein one could "come back" as a splendid tiger, an elegant snow leopard, or even the "King of Beasts," a majestic lion. My faith in those days was so intense that I burst into tears. The poor woman was dumbfounded when she saw how agitated I had become. Fighting for breath, I told her, "If I ever come back, I would like to return as a person."

RIOPELLE, JEAN-PAUL: I admire the way this great artist, fourteen years older than me, scans everything that comes into his sight with wide-open eyes. He is a man who can never have too much reality. His canvases are alive with pure colour and pure energy. I wish I could draw like him. I have been temped to write him, to ask how he came to dedicate himself to the profession of artist.

"Why did you have to leave Quebec and Canada?" I would also like to inquire. "Why do you have to live in Paris? Is Canada inhospitable to those possessed of an artistic temperament?" He would think me demented and not bother to respond.

What, indeed, would he consider me? A lunatic madman in the attic? If he did respond, he would have reminded me that he wrote to Premier Duplessis in 1948 telling him that both Canada and Quebec were too isolated from the rest of the world. "You must open up," he had demanded. Of course, his plea was ignored.

ROBBERIES: There has been a spate of them recently. The perpetrators are a gang of French-speaking louts (a teller overheard them mumbling to themselves). Unfortunately, the Toronto radio announcers — spurred on by these events — have taken to referring to Quebec in an excessively sardonic way. To them, the province is anything but beautiful because it is the breeding ground for no-good layabouts.

At the Bank yesterday, I could not help but overhear — they were speaking so loudly — Constance and Mary, another teller, exchanging prejudices.

"They don't want to work."

"Stealing is their preferred method of employment."

"I don't want to be shot by one of them."

"That gang probably isn't smart enough to use real guns."

Normally, I would have paid no attention to such outpourings, but this time I snapped. "I am fed up with listening to you mouth off your fucking, ignorant prejudices!"

The two women were astonished. Here was mild-mannered Étienne expressing an opinion. They exchanged wary glances with each other, shrugged their shoulders and retreated into silence.

ROMANTIC: Tante Isabelle often refers to herself as a "hopeless romantic." At such times, she becomes intoxicated with the idea of passion. "I am in love with the idea of love. I know there is a man out there who is my soulmate, a true kindred spirit. When I meet him, my long search will be over. I shall at long last have a home of my own and be no longer tied to Mother. My life will consist of love and freedom, the supreme elements that make up happiness."

Patiently, Madame Beaulieu explains to her sister that she could have taken seriously one or two of the many proposals bestowed on her. Her sibling responds fiercely: "Why should I have given those dusty souls houseroom? If I had done so, I would have wound up like you, married to a man who is not worthy to kiss the hem of my dress." On such occasions, Madame Beaulieu, demonstrating the tremendous patience she exercises with everyone, changes the subject or excuses herself in order to attend to some "small" domestic chore.

ROSEATE SPOONBILLS: Those creatures prove to my complete satisfaction that there must be a Creator, one with both a soaring imagination and a deft sense of humour.

I have seen a stuffed specimen at the Royal Ontario Museum, although its feathers looked dusty, shop-worn and perhaps moth-infested; it no longer possessed the dark and light hues of pink that one sees in the Audubon engravings.

Like a flamingo, a spoonbill is a ridiculous-looking animal: its huge, awkward-shaped bill and plump body render it ungainly — it is amazing that it can take to the air. And yet those beings, in their defiance of all the claims of ordinary beauty, reassure us that even the most ridiculous of us have seeds of greatness within — if we but snare them.

ROWENA: A woman of icy coldness. I liked *Ivanhoe* well enough as a *Classics Illustrated*, but the real thing — Scott's novel — left me unengaged. The movie was a slightly different story. Robert Taylor in the title role and Joan Fontaine as Rowena were entirely predictable. According to the movie magazines, Elizabeth Taylor was furious at being refused the part of the icy-looking Rowena and having to settle for what she called a "thankless" role as the voluptuous dark-haired Rebecca, the Jewess. Her anger must have seeped into her performance because I could not take my eyes away from her during the few times she was on screen. Maybe she won by not winning?

RUFFLE: Our lives were disrupted in the most pleasant way possible in the autumn of 1966. Madame B was to have another child. All of us hoped that she would finally be blessed with a little girl. Frank was as pleased as he could be. Madame B shared this feeling, but she was, as she told me, much too old, at the age of forty-five, to have another baby. "I thought I was past the time that any such happening could overtake me." She then smiled at the cumbersome way she expressed herself. In reality, she was overjoyed. The possibility of having a daughter infused her with an even stronger sense of purpose. She had so much energy that she never considered the possibility of taking the afternoon naps recommended by her doctor. She had no need of rest, she assured me.

RUNAWAY:

October 12, 1966

Dearest Étienne,

I left Canada for Japan in October 1945. After the bombing of Hiroshima and Nagasaki in August 1945, I became preoccupied with reading everything I could about that calamity. Before, I had given no thought whatsoever to the absurdity of labelling the Japanese in my mind as "monkey men" or "jaundiced baboons." Like many others I had been terrified that the Nazis or the Yellow Peril (or both) would invade and take over Canada.

When that possibility was erased and I saw what radiation had done to thousands of innocents, something in me broke. I decided that I should use my knowledge to help those unfortunate people. Within a few months I had obtained leave from my job, said goodbye to my mother, sold my possessions and

made contact with a charitable agency in Tokyo that assured
me that it would place me where my help would be of most
assistance.

My various air flights en route to Tokyo were uneventful
and tedious. Although I knew Tokyo had been hard hit by
bombings, I was astounded by what I saw as the plane came
over the Sumida River: huge chunks of the city had simply
vanished, completely levelled. Even my haphazard aerial view
revealed that many of the bombed-out parcels of land had
been turned into vegetable gardens.

I had been briefed of a mighty plague: cholera, typhus,
diphtheria, meningitis, polio and encephalitis were rampant.
I had been warned of the physical devastation. What surprised
me was the presence everywhere I turned of the panpan —
the garish, hard-nosed women who served as prostitutes to the
American servicemen.

As a child, I had read some accounts of Meiji Japan, and
I had expected that some remnants of that past glory would
assert themselves. Instead, the great temples I had read about
were funereal rather than celebratory. Everyone — the
Japanese and the GIs — moved deliberately, almost robot-like,
on the streets. This was the land of despair.

What caught my eye from the outset were the homeless
children who wandered the streets day and night. They lived
in railroad stations, under railway trestles and overpasses,
and in abandoned ruins. To support themselves, they shined
shoes, sold newspapers, recycled cigarette butts, and sold
counterfeit food coupons. Most of them begged — many of
them stole. The charin kids were expert pickpockets. Most of

the girls worked as prostitutes. The police routinely rounded up these children and placed them in detention centres, where they were subjected to every kind of physical and mental abuse. Some of the children were kept naked to prevent them from escaping.

When I arrived, I was scheduled to spend two weeks getting oriented in Tokyo. I never made it to either Hiroshima or Nagasaki. In fact, to this day, I have not visited either city. I asked if I could possibly work with the street children of Tokyo. I was told that this was impossible, but I was informed that the large White Chrysanthemum Orphanage, near Ueno Park, was desperately in need of a full-time doctor.

I have been here now for fifteen years. I know almost everything there is to know about childhood ailments. I do not know, however, how to cure a broken heart. Many of the orphans recover quickly, but most of them cannot adequately deal with the sense of abandonment. Why did their parents die? Why did their parents leave them? Sometimes the children accuse themselves of incompetence. "If I had been a good child, I would have at least one parent," many tell themselves. "There is something wrong with me," others accuse themselves.

My work may have given me a sense of purpose but in recent years I am crippled by the certainty that you probably accuse yourself daily of the crimes to which so many of the orphans subject themselves. That is why I have written. I comfort myself with the possibility that you may have some interest in knowing me.

RUPTURE: Like all motherless children, I had spent countless hours daydreaming about my long-absent parent. What did she look like? What kind of a person was she? Why had she left me behind? The person constructed in my mind was highly idealized. Of course, I also despised that same person for ridding herself of me.

Now I had to confront reality. My mother may have been a selfless person in the service of other children, but she had not cared about her own child.

Now that the possibility of seeing this imaginary person has become a distinct possibility, I feel shattered. I much prefer, I realize, the comfortable world of my imagination to that of dire reality. I do not wish even more precious, demanding Time to be consumed thinking about her.

S

The shape of **S** probably comes from the shape of an archer's bow. Whatever its source, it is sinewy and sensuous, incorporating the spiritual and the sexual in its serpentine curve. Since it is the primary sibilant in English, it is associated with some obnoxious sounds like shoo, shush and shut-up.

SEPARATION: The most gut-wrenching emotions that human beings can experience occur at the death of a loved one. There are also the moments of intense agony when one truly realizes that Time brings an end to all living things.

SEPARATISM: Sometimes — as in **SEPARATION** above — this alternative seems to be the only genuine solution for Quebec. However, as soon as this possibility is mooted, French-

Canadians are told by the federal government and newspaper editorials that they are an essential ingredient in that mixture of mongrel areas constituting Confederation. No English politician ever waxes sentimental about la belle province; no English person states that they share any affinity with the French-Canadians; no affection of any kind is expressed. We are necessary because we are owned lock, stock and barrel. Of course, what landlord in his right mind would give away a valuable piece of property? In turn, French-Canadians grow angrier.

SERENE: The feeling of bliss, of happiness expected and received. That is how we feel about Anna, who was born this April 1967. Such a perfect little beauty. She seems to know that we all belong to her, are eager worshippers at her shrine. Madame B refers to her as "my miracle." The baby smiled at the age of seven weeks. Not just a smile — a wide, mirthful gleam takes over her face. When she looks at me, she seems enchanted.

SNAKES AND LADDERS: We played this board game in the Orphanage for hours on end. Even as a child, despite the anxiety aroused by the constant falls, I found this a worthwhile pastime, perhaps because life itself consists of the occasional step up (the illusion of getting somewhere or reaching a goal) and many setbacks (disappointments, frustrations). A much more virtuous activity than *Monopoly*, which invites each player to outwit his competitors and, in the process, impoverish them.

SOPHISTICATION: The Greek root for this word is the same as for **SOPHIST**. The **sophist** is someone of considerable intelligence and cunning who loves to mount clever but fallacious arguments. Such people take pleasure in manipulating the truth in instances where they know what they are proposing is inherently false. A **sophisticate** is someone with a complex, nuanced attitude. Many **sophisticates** are **sophists**.

My resentment of sophisticates and sophists stems from the fact that I do not possess any of their skills in dealing with the world. I am simply someone who lacks the ability to play some very necessary games in the struggle to survive.

SORROW: His net is impossible to evade. I have just had a brief note from one of my mother's colleagues.

Your mother collapsed the other day. We had all noticed that she was a bit more care-worn than usual these past few months. We have been hard pressed to raise funds for the Orphanage, and, as usual, she took these matters personally, as if she somehow was responsible for the approaching catastrophe. We were flummoxed when she fell to the ground in a dead faint. Subsequent investigation has revealed that she has a serious heart problem, one which cannot be operated on. Although she knows that she does not have long to live, her spirits are cheerful.

Beatrice has always been a person who keeps very much to herself. I did not know of your existence until she took me into her confidence this morning and asked me to write. She is very anxious to know if you can make the journey to Tokyo to see her. It would mean a great deal to her to see you. Phone me as soon as you receive this letter. Your mother will reimburse you for the flight. She also wishes you to purchase a camera so

that you can record what Tokyo looks like. She is certain that
your bad fortune in Shanghai will not happen here. Beatrice
laments that she has never given you a single present — she
is anxious to remedy this deficiency. Finally, she is deeply
touched that she is one of the two persons you have told
about your drawings. Can you bring some with you?

The letter took six days to reach me. That afternoon I enquired about air tickets and made a tentative booking. I then called my mother's colleague. The poor woman could hardly speak: my mother had died that night.

STORKS: Large, ungainly members of the bird family, but I, and all the other orphans I knew, venerated them. They had the reputation of delivering babies to loving mothers and fathers whereas we had never been carried on such journeys.

STRAITLACED: A label that many people affix to me. At the Bank I always wear a crisply pressed dark suit, a narrow single-colour tie, a white shirt and highly polished black shoes. Since my costume is so institutional, many of my colleagues assume I am simply a man in a grey flannel suit.

Madame Beaulieu does not know the expression *straitlaced*, but she has a penchant for calling pompous, overly correct people *stuffed shirts*. I once told her that some people might apply such a noun to me; I also defined *straitlaced* for her. She gave me one of her soft, caressing smiles. "No one who truly knows you would ever think of such words to describe you. People who are *sympathique* do not suffer such afflictions."

STRAY: Poor, pathetic little Vincent — three years younger than me — clung to me constantly. He would cry sometimes when he could not be with me. He so much wanted an elder bother. He was not transferred to Toronto because he ran away just before we left. Even more shy and withdrawn than I, he beheld in me a kindred spirit.

T

T is a vainglorious creature, one that insists that its two vertical ends be given "star" treatment. The T does this because it knows in reality that it is simply a form of x.

Looks are deceiving, the T reminds us, and uneasy is the head that wears the crown. This letter is also wary of its place towards the end of the alphabet — there is an autumnal aspect to its personality as it awaits the grim prospect of winter and old age.

A TALE OF TWO CITIES: In Dickens' view, a contrast between violence-strewn, ruffian-filled Paris and heady, freedom-loving London. In my mind, the disparity is between the grey cityscape of Toronto and the boisterous, beautiful boulevards of Montreal. The former is built upon day-to-day knowledge whereas the latter is the creature of memory and, of course, romanticized and therefore distorted.

There are no Montreal drawings. In my cityscapes, Toronto has a complicated personality: cheerful, capricious, sombre, sullen, seedy and, sometimes, majestic. Like any person, a city has good and dark sides accompanied by a wide variety of moods.

TIME: My greatest friend — my ferocious enemy. Time allows me to forget the injuries of the past — soften the hurt feelings and mend the wounds. Yet it will also vanquish me. We are, after all, allotted only so many days in the lottery euphemistically called life.

TIMOTHY WALLINGFORD: What a strange man he is! He looks the same as he did twenty years ago — time has yet to catch up with him. Of medium height and build, he has delicate features. His deep brown eyes remain hidden behind horn-rimmed glasses. As before, his hair is an even, dark colour, although he has piebald spotting on the back of his head. Otherwise, no evidence of white or grey. He did not remember me when I dealt with him at the Bank almost five years ago.

He has the strangest story of any of the orphans I knew. From what I have been able to piece together, he was born in Toronto to parents of considerable inherited wealth. An only child, his early years were idyllic. He was doted upon by both parents, although from infancy he claims to have been aware that his father's only real joy in life resided in his wife. Timothy was acceptable to his father because he was cherished by his mother. In this way, he was, as he put it, protected.

Things came to a sorry pass one day when Timothy's parents were out shopping. The six-year-old spent a stressful morning under the tutelage of his governess. The child was worried about his mother's safety. He told his caretaker that he had dreamed the previous night that mama had died. The governess, a young Swedish woman possessing a sweet temperament, did her best to assuage the child's sense of foreboding. Nothing would happen to her, she assured him over and over again. The child's apprehension was not alleviated.

Finally, at noon, husband and wife arrived home. Although it was not customary for her to allow the child to rush out the front door to greet his parents, Ingrid broke her own rule on this day, happy to allow Timothy to see for himself how groundless his worries had been.

As soon as the child made his way out the door, he ran in the direction of his mother. His greeting — louder than usual — startled her. She lost her balance, fell to the ground and hit her head. She died instantly. There was not a spot of blood on her face. She looked like a sleeping angel, her son recalled.

From that day onwards, Mr. Wallingford harboured a deep animosity for his son, although he never addressed a single word to him in remonstration about the catastrophe itself. A few weeks later, Mr. Williams informed his son that he had determined to take up residency in Europe. That was when Timothy was placed in the Orphanage.

As boy and man, Timothy had never been able to reach any kind of conclusion to the question that haunted him. Had his father disliked but tolerated him before his mother's death? Or had his father sought to revenge himself on his wife's murderer?

There was — as is often the case in such situations — a third option: the father had always hated the child and that hatred had been exacerbated by the incidents leading to his wife's death.

When I saw him last, Timothy's face was that of a man torn apart by guilt and shame. Deep etched lines crisscrossed his face vertically and horizontally. His eyes were so hooded that it was difficult to see that they were an unusual bright purple. His cheeks were drawn in, as if he has just taken in a huge amount of air. Well over six feet in height, he carried himself so poorly that as an adult he looked, like myself, below average height.

Trained in political economy at the University of Toronto, Timothy became what I call a Captain of Industry. The notice of his death in yesterday's *Telegram* mentioned that he had no living relatives and stated that he had died suddenly and unexpectedly. I am certain he took his own life.

TRADING CARDS: Comic books may have been forbidden at the Orphanage, but the nuns were not completely iconoclastic. Some of the boys collected hockey cards whereas many girls had pictures of animals. I avoided both forms of collecting. I wasn't interested in photographs of men with missing teeth, and I found poodles, dyed pink and festooned with ribbons, repulsive.

TRANSIENT: As in here today, gone tomorrow. There are also transients, people whose lives are experienced completely on the edge of society.

Three months ago, a man began coming to the New Yorker

cinema on Yonge Street, always arriving just as the film was about to begin. After half an hour he would scream invectives at the actors and dare them to walk down from the screen and confront him. Such outbursts were brief, and he would issue them, rise to his feet and walk angrily down the aisle to exit the theatre. In this way, he avoided being expelled by the management. After a while, the patrons of the cinema seemed to look forward to this curious performance.

I witnessed four or five such episodes but did not think much of them. Just as I was arriving yesterday to see *The 400 Blows*, I noticed the same person on the street. Dressed in a frayed grey suit with a fedora perched uncertainly on his head, he would walk about ten or fifteen feet, stop abruptly, make a moaning sound, and then walk back to the spot where he had begun. He would repeat this action over and over. I thought of the labours of Sisyphus and lamented this fellow's obsessive need to repeat his past so often and so furiously. I had to walk close to him in order to make my way into the foyer and only then did I recognize the carbuncular face of my old enemy, Fred.

Another figure from the past caught up with me today, this time in the *Telegram*, the only newspaper our branch of the Royal takes in. There was a crime story, related in a salacious style for which the periodical is known, about Mr. Sanders, who had been murdered in Brazil. After being dismissed by the Royal and spending about two years at the men's prison in Kingston, he had become involved in some scheme to pilfer the coffers of wealthy widows. He had been "on the lam" in South America after "pulling off" a number of such thefts but had been "bumped off" by gangsters whom he had defrauded. The brief report was accompanied by a photograph of my former boss sprawled on the sidewalk of a street in Rio.

TREVI FOUNTAIN: I was not sophisticated enough to admire *La Dolce Vita*. I felt badly for the children murdered by their demented father, but Anita Ekberg's cavorting in the Trevi Fountain captivated me. I found all kinds of photographs of that wonder in the picture collection of the library. Muscular but energetic Oceanus, the tritons and the horses filled my imagination. How I wanted to visit Rome, seek out the fountain, witness the conquest of water by Oceanus, throw coins in the water and make some wishes.

TRUTH: Impossible to discover. Impenetrable. May not exist.

Sorrow is everywhere. Of that I am certain.

Anna reached her third month in June 1967, although Madame Beaulieu always speaks in terms of weeks. "She is precocious, my tiny one. She smiled at three weeks — none of the boys reached that milestone so early." At eight weeks she held her neck up decisively when being held and moved it so that she could look at everyone and everything in a room. At eleven weeks she knew the members of her family, including me, and began to make shy with others.

That summer I did something unusual for me — a real break in my routine. I left the Bank every afternoon at the earliest opportunity, rushed home and played with the baby as soon as she had finished her nap. Madame Beaulieu could then go out on small errands while I lavished my undivided attention on Anna, who was always delighted to settle in my arms.

I shall never forget that day: June 21. I arrived home that Wednesday afternoon at the usual time, expecting that my land-lady and the baby would be waiting for me in the living room. No one was there. I walked upstairs to the nursery, but the crib was empty. I knocked at Madame B's bedroom. She came to the door, tears pouring down her cheek. The baby was gone, taken to hospital by ambulance ten minutes before.

Madame B could hardly speak: "They told me that it was a crib death. She died during her afternoon nap. She was perfectly happy when I put her down, gave me her usual big smile and then fell asleep. I could not awaken her an hour later. I was here, taking a nap next to her in this bed, when she died. She died right here." She pointed to the small lump near where she had been sleeping. "I cannot believe, Étienne, that the Saviour could be so cruel to me." She hugged me, asked me to stay with her until Frank, whom she had phoned, returned home.

U

U: Is it simply a rounded-off V or a member of the alphabet in its own right? Many serious self-esteem issues here.

UCCELLO, PAOLO: I hope my drawings might someday give others the kind of pleasure Uccello's brightly coloured people and horses have given me. This well-educated early Renaissance artist had the soul of child. His wonder at the beauties of the world can be seen in every line he drew and painted.

UN: This prefix unmakes the meaning of all the words to which it is affixed. If something was once X, it becomes non-X once *un* is attached to it. If someone is creative, they can become uncreative. So much power in those two letters.

Anna came into existence and her beautiful existence was quickly and unfairly savaged by Time. My Mother was a comparatively young woman when she died.

UNENDURABLE: I was not completely unprepared for the letter postmarked "Munich" that arrived two days after Anna's death. One of Chang's friends, now in the foreign service, wrote to tell me that "a mutual friend no longer will see the light of day. I am not at liberty to tell you of the circumstances under which he reached oblivion, but I can tell you the manner caused me considerable distress. Burn this letter as soon as you read it. Remember: I never wrote to you."

So I shall never know how my friend met his end. I doubt he died of any natural cause. I think my correspondent is indicating that fact to me in his circuitous way. Chang had a strong, independent disposition. He could not abide conformity; he was the enemy of deceit; he felt that the "Chinese spirit" was being crushed by Mao.

Was he arrested in the middle of the night, taken to a vacant lot in the countryside and machine-gunned? Was he tried by some sort of kangaroo court and then hanged? Was he starved to death? Was he given a decent burial or just thrown unceremoniously into the ground like a dog? Whatever the actual facts may be of his death, Chang's spirit seems alive in me, as if I have become the repository of his deepest feelings and aspirations.

Chang was my age. We are so quickly undone.

UNREAL: The true realm of the artist, a strange place off-limits to most mortal beings.

V

V: the two lines begin apart and then conjoin. There is a tranquil beauty to this shape, giving the illusion that all difficulties, no matter how great, can be resolved.

VANISH: We appear and then we disappear. This is the nature of human existence, as in "Here today, gone tomorrow." The artist may have trouble reaching the "truth" in any work of art, but the work of art is eternal — its creator ephemeral.

Perhaps that is why I have finally become a portraitist. I require some way to reconstitute the dead — my Mother, Anna, Chang. Now there are pictures of my mother staring out harshly or beseechingly or imploringly or shyly.

The baby's eyes twinkle in most of the pictures I have made of her. Sometimes her countenance is suffused with an intelligent sadness, as if she knew that she would spend very little time in this vale of sadness. Sometimes she is a ghost, her face and clothes completely translucent.

Chang is a strong force in all the pictures I have made of him. He exhibits himself proudly in many; he looks menacingly at the viewer in others; in profile he is a man of irresolute, strong opinions.

With my mother, I have no photographs to work from. In the drawings, she is completely the creature of my imagination. There are no photographs of Anna, and I do not know how accurate my memory is of what she looked like, even though I held her countless times and looked admiringly at her tiny countenance. So many years have passed since I saw Chang that I am not sure I accurately remember his appearance, either.

Do these portraits help me to cope with those who have been cruelly snatched from me? I am not sure they do. As soon as I complete one version of Chang, I am compelled to undertake another.

I can never get any of these people right. I have set myself impossible tasks. As soon as I think I have achieved a genuine likeness, that sense of certainty vanishes. And so I must begin again on yet another attempt to capture the "truth" of the person I am rendering.

Then there are the orphans: Virginie, Timothy, Fred, Émile and all the others. Sometimes they appear melancholic and withdrawn, but, more often than not, their faces are filled with an exuberance of which I do not have a clear memory.

VENEER: Children seldom see the need of applying such a coating to their personalities. As adults, the veneer protects them from the onslaughts of the world.

VERMEER, JOHANNES: Evidently, the great artist painted few pictures. Many of the known "Vermeers" are fakes. If someone owned and loved a Vermeer, would that love be killed by the announcement that it was a fake? If love died in such circumstances, was it ever genuine? Or did it reside simply in the pride of possession? In moments of hubris, I wonder if, were my feeble attempts ever discovered, anyone would, in subsequent years, attempt to "imitate" me.

VERSIMILITUDE: The necessary stepping stone between the artist and the world. People and places do not have to be rendered realistically (as they look to the eye), but the creator must have the wherewithal to make his inner world speak to the inner worlds of an audience.

VERY: Adjective/adverb best avoided. The majority of human experiences are good or bad; extremes are not rare, but it is best not to accentuate either in the event one's hubris draws the anger of the gods.

VINCENT: None of the various branches of the Bank at which I have been assigned have been robbed while I worked at them. I have become a kind of good-luck mascot: no one will attempt a heist while Étienne is with us, they say.

My luck changed two months ago at noon when I was the

only teller on duty. A scruffy, wasted-looking man handed me a note informing me that I was to hand over everything in my till. When I looked up, he had a gun in his hand.

As I searched the thief's face, I recognized Vincent Gélinas, who had been at the Hôtel Dieu in Montreal. He obviously did not remember me.

I looked him straight in the eye, and I was certain that this was the first time he had attempted an armed robbery. Time had not hardened his face, which still bore traces of innocence. Looking around the room, I realized that no one was aware of what was going on. Speaking in French, I told the thief that I knew a toy gun when I saw one, and I suggested that he put it away. Astounded by my perspicacity (I really did not know if my assumption was correct or not), he did what he was told.

He stood there, looking at me. I could see both fright and desperation in his eyes. He may well have been on the verge of tears.

Knowing that no one could possibly have the slightest idea of what we were saying, I told him that robbing banks with even a fake gun would soon lead him to either death or incarceration. He nodded in agreement, confirming my suspicion that he had never before wandered down such a foolish path. In the best imitation of fatherly conduct I could muster, I told him that he would have to find employment.

I could see that he saw the wisdom of such counsel. Again making sure that no one could see me, I removed two hundred dollars from my till, handed it to him and requested that he return the loan to me when he was back on his feet. He furtively acknowledged his thanks and left.

A few minutes later, I removed four fifty-dollar bills from my wallet and placed it in my till. I thought that would be the end of the story until yesterday at noon when Vincent, a cheerful smile on his face, returned, walked up to me and announced that he wanted to make a deposit. That is the only loan I have negotiated in all my years with the Royal.

W is the widest of all the letters. It is extremely proud of its apex and insists that it is always rendered with due majesty and solemnity. My Ws are always a deep purple, in keeping with the royal status of this member of the alphabet.

In the last two months, the letters and words have attached themselves to my eyes with new vigour. Almost as if I have been given a new kind of sight. The blues are far richer and deeper, the reds are more intense, the yellows are sunlike in intensity, the oranges are burnt deeply, the greens are colours of nature I have never beheld before.

WATER: As a child in Montreal, I dreamed of water constantly. In some I would be gliding through soft blue currents. In others I would be swimming from small island to small island. Once or twice, I would dive down to a dry spot on the ocean floor, re-emerge, and then go through the entire process again.

When I arrived in Toronto, those dreams ceased. In the past two months, they have returned. Nowadays, I am sitting beside a tranquil, resplendent, forest-green lake. The water is so inviting that I wander in and submerge myself. With the self-assurance of a seal or porpoise, I scurry through the water. The fish, in a wide assortment of shapes and vivid colours, do not move to get out of my way. They obviously know I am a kindred spirit. When I awake in the morning, I feel thoroughly revitalized.

WEASEL: Their fur may be soft to the touch and their colours alluring, but these are treacherous creatures. I recall how the supreme trickster, the wily Jacob — with the assistance of his mother — stole his twin brother Esau's birthright by smearing his smooth skin with goat's hair so that his blind father, Isaac, would confer his blessing upon him.

Weasels are synonymous with deceit, trickery and false promises. When I began my drawings ten years ago, I promised myself no portraits of any kind because the genre is subject to those awful vices. A landscape is a view — real or imaginary. People are vainglorious, unduly complicated and, ultimately, beyond understanding. Why should I subject myself to such a dubious enterprise as putting them on paper?

And yet, in the past two months I have completed about fifty portraits. None are from life — some from photographs, many from memory, others purely from my imagination.

The other day I asked Madame Beaulieu if I might leaf through her albums and perhaps borrow a few snapshots. She assented at once. So now there are individual portraits of the five family members — even some of them seated at table or their arms around each other at a family gathering.

The dead remain my real subjects. In those of my mother she looks excessively beautiful, fragile even. In others she glances haughtily at the viewer. Sometimes she is angry; she is also beseeching, almost plaintive; in many she is frightened, afraid of being alone and abandoned.

Then there are portraits of Chang. In some he looks remarkably robust. His jet black hair bristles with energy. He looks confidently at the spectator. In others his skin is a dark grey patina with worry lines affixed.

Anna is a beautiful child in my drawings. Her eyes look wistfully, sometimes beseechingly, but she is the embodiment of courage. There is a wonderful defiance in her look.

I have tried to give permanent existences to these three persons, rescue them from oblivion. How is this possible? How, I ask myself, can I draw these people who have been taken away from me?

I am obviously trying to cheat Death. Surrounded by that ghastly force, I am consumed with the desire to live. I assemble these ghosts as talismans to ward him off.

If I am in mourning for my mother, Chang and Anna, why isn't my new work filled with a black despair? Instead, the new drawings are infused with a riot of bright colours. Every time I set out to capture Despair, he evades me. Why does Hope insist in asserting itself?

THE WINGS OF THE DOVE: Like Mark Twain, Henry James was fascinated by orphans. In Huckleberry Finn and Tom

Sawyer, Twain created mischievous adolescents who ultimately right themselves. James is not so optimistic. In *The Portrait of a Lady*, Isabel Archer falls into the clutches of those two embodiments of duplicity: Gilbert Osmond and his mistress Madame Merle.

Milly Theale in *The Wings of the Dove* is "isolated, un-mothered, and unguarded." She has great wealth but is so emotionally destitute that she is ensnared by two gold-diggers, Kate Croy and Merton Densher. When she learns that she has been betrayed by this pair, Milly, who is dying of tuberculosis, turns her head to the wall and dies. James, who was not an orphan, nevertheless understood the condition well.

THE WIZARD OF OZ: I was seven years old when we were carted off to see that film. The nuns told us that the movie would entrance us with its story of a magical journey. I remember being frightened when the house takes off in black and white and immensely relieved when it lands in colour. Billie Burke melted my heart; her Queen Glinda was so kind and gentle to the wayfarers. I didn't mind Dorothy or the Cowardly Lion. I had my doubts about the other pilgrims.

I might have settled into the film, but the maliciousness of the Wicked Witch disturbed me. So this is pure evil? I must have asked myself. Then her flying monkeys, their ugly, wide countenances agleam with menace, began their mission of pillage and destruction. I became so frightened I wet myself.

I looked around, but no one else in the audience seemed the least bit bothered. I told myself to get a grip on my fear. I suppose I did so, but I then became anxious for the movie to end.

I was not relieved when I learned that the Wizard — supposedly a person of power — was Frank Morgan.

For me the picture had no happy ending. Another instance of life's many disappointments conjoined with moments of sheer terror. I was happy to walk out of the theatre and onto the icy sidewalk. I was also relieved that my trousers did not show that I had peed them.

WORDS: Separate us from all other creatures. Although we employ them to describe our thoughts and experiences, we often regret this ability since words have the capacity to make us aware of the trials and tribulations of being human. I use words, therefore I suffer.

I reluctantly decided to inform my mother about the existence of my drawings. If my mother loves me, she will unconditionally accept my chosen way of life, I told myself. She cherished my words about my new profession.

WRITER: Manipulator of words. Someone who exchanges the relative comfort of reading for the precarious and dubious one — as I now know — of giving others something to read.

X may mark the spot, but it has a wide assortment of personal problems. First of all, it is, with Y, overused in algebra. Then there are the mutant superheroic X-men, rather shabby creatures in my opinion. Then, all bad products in advertisements — for the purpose of negative comparison to a name product — are Brand X. This letter has had the misfortune to associate itself with things forbidden or depraved.

X-RAYS: A lot of people are frightened of X-rays, which might reveal that something in the body is diseased. The resulting images look into the body searching for something wrong. Yet the inner secrets revealed might lead to a cure. I have recently begun to draw such images, incursions into the realities lying beneath surfaces.

Negatives are forms of x-rays. Once, Chang insisted on taking my rolls to be developed. I demurred, but he insisted. A few days later he told me that he had something to show me. He returned with a large sheaf of papers separated into two piles. One contained the exposed negatives, the others the prints made from them. He handed them to me. He expressed no emotion. I was certain he disliked what he had seen. I leafed my way through both piles. Nothing had turned out as I had expected. Chang broke the silence. "These photographs are masterful. You have a curious eye, and you have forced me to see Shanghai in a new way."

Y

Y lives in a state of complete confusion. Is it a vowel or a consonant? Many ego problems here.

YEARNING: Madame Beaulieu is still having a difficult time coping. "Anna was such a happy baby. She beamed smiles at everyone from the time she was a month old. Never a sign of bad health. Rosy cheeks. Angelic bow-shaped lips." She begins crying again, but this time the sound is more muted, a bit more accepting of the tragedy.

I shall never forget the funeral and its aftermath. Frail Madame Beaupré remained behind in Montreal. When Isabelle arrived, the sisters embraced, Frank pecked his sister-in-law's cheek and the three boys kissed their aunt enthusiastically. Isabelle offered me her hand, as if I were to kiss it.

A weary silence soon overtook the seven of us. Isabelle asked her sister what the autopsy revealed. Madame Beaulieu shrugged her shoulders: "Crib death."

Tante Isabelle nodded but obviously expected her sister to say more. "There is no more to tell. The baby looked the picture of health. She never cried."

"That should have been a warning to you. Healthy children cry all the time for attention. There was obviously something wrong with Anna."

Madame Beaulieu directed a steely look in her sister's direction but held her tongue. Then Isabelle switched her line of interrogation. "Of course, you baptized the baby. She will live in the company of the saints awaiting our arrival."

Startled, Madame Beaulieu responded: "You are well aware that her baptism was scheduled for next week. You were coming down for it."

"But you took the precaution of baptizing her privately well before that public event, didn't you? Most people do that nowadays."

"I did no such thing. I saw no need."

Isabelle's face was now scarlet. "You saw no need? The little soul is now doomed to spend all eternity in Limbo with all the unbelievers who have never had the sacrament of Baptism bestowed on them."

Never before had I seen Madame Beaulieu display even the slightest display of anger to her sibling. Drawing her breath in, she looked over at Isabelle. "You are a superstition-ridden old biddy! You will never mention this matter to me again." Isabelle burst into tears and left the room. The five of us — all amazed at the acrimony unleashed — looked in the direction of the speaker, who seemed unaware of the enormity of the gulf she had opened up between her sister and herself.

The two women exchanged hardly any words at the funeral or the gathering at the Beaulieu house afterwards. After all the mourners had taken their leave, Isabelle announced that the family would say the rosary together. "You may go upstairs to your room, Étienne," she instructed me. Madame Beaulieu abruptly stood up: "We are not doing any such thing, Isabelle. Frank and I wish Étienne to remain here with us. We consider him a member of this family. He is one of our sons."

If Isabelle was astonished, she did not show it. She did not burst into tears, either. She quickly went to her room and left for Montreal early the next morning.

I was not surprised by Madame Beaulieu's declaration. Only on reflection, however, did I fully comprehend the significance of what she meant. That evening, as I rose to my feet after the recitation of the rosary, she called me aside and pointed in the direction of the kitchen. Once the door to that room was securely closed, she told me that henceforth I should never address her again as Madame Beaulieu. "You may call me by my given name — Beatrice. If you wish, I would like you to address me as Maman."

Z

Z is one of the alphabet's problem children. Maybe Shakespeare's Duke of Kent got it right: "Thou whoreson zed, thou unnecessary letter!" Z's problems in the English-speaking world are renowned. Americans insist on *zee* whereas English-speaking Canadians somewhat pompously insist on *zed*. "It's the only thing that makes us different from Americans," one teller summarily informed me. I decided not to argue with him.

Z is also the last letter in the alphabet. Even the alphabet comes to an end.

ZEST: An appetite for life. If someone should inadvertently read this diary, would they apply this noun to describe me? I fervently hope so.

ZIGZAG: Life is a series of abrupt right and left turns. There is no clear path, as Dante informs us:

> *Midway upon the journey of life*
> *I found myself in a wood so dark,*
> *That I couldn't tell where the straight path lay.*

ZODIAC: A complete circuit. The compass of eternity.

This evening, time seems, for some strange reason, to be running out. Words are fleeing me. I cannot write. Why is this ability abandoning me? Perhaps I have said all I am capable of? Will I still be able to make my drawings? What, I am forced to ask, would the world be like without the existence of Étienne? I do not wish a response to this question.

I've always been attracted to the metaphor of time's winged chariot, but I do not want this trope to overtake me just yet. I have a great deal of work remaining. I must, for example, begin a series of self-portraits. I have never wanted to study myself in the mirror, but the time has arrived to capture reflections of that curious person, Étienne Morneau.

Never before have I so much wanted to be alive. I feel fire and music under my feet. The world is a pure, cool green charged with the glory of existence. I am intoxicated with it, as if I have finally swallowed its essence. I feel an energy I did not know I possessed. I am rampant with images. They float in front of me, demanding I bring them to life.

[EDITOR'S NOTE: When Madame Beaulieu discovered Étienne's lifeless body, she was obviously badly shaken, but she noticed that his face was suffused, as it had been so often in life, with an angelic smile. She sat down on his bed and took one of his outstretched hands in hers. To her surprise it was not cold — it felt almost hot. Although overcome with sorrow, she was certain he had passed away in the midst of a happy dream. Perhaps, she told me, he had been welcomed to the Gates of Paradise by Anna or Chang or, she fervently hoped, his Mother.]